A NOBLE PROFESSION

OTHER BOOKS BY PIERRE BOULLE
The Bridge Over the River Kwai
Not the Glory
Face of a Hero
The Test
S.O.P.H.I.A.

The Vanguard Press, Inc. · *New York*

A NOBLE PROFESSION

by *Pierre Boulle*

Author of "THE BRIDGE OVER THE RIVER KWAI"

Translated from the French

by Xan Fielding

Second Printing

Copyright, ©, 1960, by Pierre Boulle
No portion of this book may be reproduced in any
form without the written permission of the pub-
lisher, except by a reviewer who may wish to quote
brief passages in connection with a review for a
newspaper or magazine.
Library of Congress Card Catalogue Number: 60–
15063

Manufactured in the United States of America by
H. Wolff, New York

. . . Ready to surrender himself faithfully to the claim of his own world of shades.

PART ONE

1   The human species—the main stem of this species, at least (certain offshoots that do not contribute to the central growth must be regarded as exceptions)—the human species is in the process of aspiring to a degree of intellectual loyalty beyond which it will be difficult to develop any further; for no progress can be conceived once perfection is attained, and there are countless signs to show that perfection has, in fact, been well-nigh reached in this particular field of morality, as in so many other realms.

The most striking sign of all, probably, is the feeling of disgust inspired by those stray branches that have not followed us in our constant ascent toward mental probity. We abhor any individual who does not "play the game" in that respect, and particularly anyone who tries to pass himself off as something he is not. The success of such terms as "charlatan" and "fraud," which the moralists apply to him, shows the extent of the indignation to which this despicable form of deceit gives rise, and also of the satisfaction we feel at seeing it condemned. This is because we, the normal elements of the main stem, are always true to ourselves, do not practice fraud, never use counterfeit coins, and are nauseated by the mere idea of investing ourselves with merits we do not possess—in short, because we have become intellectually *honest* in the broadest sense of the word.

When we are treated to one of those dissertations in which truth and candor triumph over turpitude and falsehood, we thank our lucky stars not only for our own moral rectitude but also for our infallible perspicacity; we feel that in this particular field we now possess such standards of judgment that no impostor can possibly delude us, that no base metal can blind us with its glitter, and that we can recognize at a glance any jackdaw in peacock's feathers. Since this wisdom of ours is relatively recent (progress during the last few years has been prodigious), our diagnosis has the strictures and lack of fine distinctions that are only to be expected in neophytes. A human being who is not all of one piece is still beyond our conception. We refuse to admit that, not fitting into any particular category, he may oscillate perpetually between duplicity and honesty without even being aware of it, and actually exhaust himself in a vain endeavor to reach a state of equilibrium.

This was not the opinion held by Dr. Fog. Dr. Fog was a man of science, a man of vast experience who had devoted a great deal of time to the study of the human brain, and who, besides his medical activities, exercised other, secret functions likewise closely connected with the mind. He maintained that this state of uncertainty, this mental instability, was perfectly feasible and, indeed, fairly common. Dr. Fog was a psychiatrist, admittedly, and specialists in this field have often been known to make pronouncements contrary to all common sense.

Be that as it may, when he met Cousin, *alias* Arvers, the doctor felt he had discovered a brain that was worth particular attention and that was admirably suited to illustrate his theories. The circumstances that led him to apply himself to this personality were at once as commonplace and exceptional as the war that had engendered them.

Cousin was an intellectual. Dr. Fog often had to underline this point, which he considered an essential factor. But to him this status did not imply belonging to a particular class of society; nor, in his view, did it necessarily proceed from any special education or distinctive upbringing. He looked upon it as the outcome of an innate, fundamental principle, the imponderable presence or absence of which produced in human beings, at birth, a differentiation as emphatic as sex. In Cousin's case, however, his profession and social background were in keeping with his character.

The son of a writer, a writer himself, born in an atmosphere of letters, brought up on a diet of letters, having absorbed at various stages of his life a considerable body of letters, he was a man of letters to his fingertips, a man of letters with his vices, his virtues, his absurdities, his noble or puerile enthusiasms, and his tendency to subordinate facts to the figments of his imagination.

At the age of thirty he had already distinguished himself in most of the fields open to a man of his calling. He had started by writing novels. In these he revealed the supreme qualities of a writer in the most brilliant manner; that is to say, he succeeded with equal felicity in enhancing reality in such a way as to endow it with the glorious hues of artistic fiction and in polishing and martialing the products of his fantasy in such a rational manner that they eventually assumed every appearance of reality.

At the end of some of his books—those in which he had given the best of himself—when he felt so moved by the final pages that he almost shed tears over certain passages, over certain words he had put into his characters' mouths, his sense of conviction and emotion were condensed into a brief formula underneath the last line: the geographical locality of his creation and the date of its achievement. Thus, *"Paris, the . . . of October, 19 . . ."* or *"Timbuktoo, January 19 . . ."* or even *"At sea, this month of June 19 . . ."* served as an outlet to his inordinate enthusiasm, and his printers never possessed any italics sufficiently forceful to do justice to this state of mind.

He tried his hand at literary criticism and met with the same success; his analytical mind pared down the works under review until there emerged a simple formula that he acclaimed as the fundamental essence of the text but which was, in fact, in every case, the reflection of his own conceptions. He also made a name for himself in journalism; while adhering faithfully to the material facts, he had an inimitable talent for investing them with some original significance that corresponded, without his being aware of it, to his intuitive conviction, to his anxiety to satisfy some higher authority or simply the requirements of his art.

He might have spent his whole life like this, following the destiny common to all men of letters, if the war had not broken out. When it did, the whole course of his existence was abruptly changed.

Paradoxically, in September, 1939, during the first days of mobilization, he experienced a violent thirst for heroism, and since his desires straightway took the form of intensive mental activity, he began to visualize and imagine himself performing outstanding feats of arms. Is thirty perhaps a critical age in a man's life, a point at which he feels an imperative need for a change? Or did his mind derive some particular fascination in contemplating himself—him, an inoffensive intellectual—winning his spurs on the field of battle; did his pride experience some subtle pleasure in dreaming that peaceful souls can, in certain circumstances, outdo professional soldiers in audacity? The nobility of this attitude could not in any case be questioned as a principle: it was that of countless Frenchmen. But Cousin's imagination swept him swiftly to the topmost summits, and in less than no time his halo was all aglow, dazzling everyone who looked at it—for in his dreams there were always a number of witnesses to his valor.

This new ambition manifested itself in the form of brightly colored visions. He pictured himself, for example, advancing into enemy territory at the head of his platoon, thrusting forward well beyond the front line—and this, furthermore, despite the strictest and most explicit orders of his superiors; for he liked to think of himself as a rather undisciplined character, a bit of a "bad egg" imbued with all sorts of good qualities that drew an indulgent smile from those indispensable witnesses to his daydreams.

His deliberate disobedience would lead to a striking victory. He would disrupt the enemy's lines of communication, cause it untold losses, and come back with a mass of prisoners. At this point he had to make up some trivial but extremely precise material details to maintain the enthusiasm of his triumphant return. The C.O. would summon him to H.Q. and address him in his stern disciplinarian's voice.

"Cousin, you have disobeyed orders. Consider yourself under open arrest."

"Yes, sir," Lieutenant Cousin would reply, standing stiffly at attention.

"And you will be mentioned in dispatches for having been so successful," the C.O. would add, changing his tone.

This type of conversation—a subconscious recollection of the adventure stories he had read as a child—made his ears ring, and each role was defined with the utmost clarity in his mind. When he came to his senses he realized how childishly hackneyed these characters were, but in less than no time he would once again succumb to their irresistible fascination.

His intellectual courage, fired by the longing to surpass everyone else, sometimes led him to the point of forcing his hero to the supreme sacrifice. This, however, did not happen very often. His mind would never reach the state of gloomy exaltation that allowed him

to envisage his own death, without first indulging in a
desperate struggle with itself. To him this was the sublime limit, to which it was almost impossible to aspire,
even in the realm of dreams. He could picture himself
without too much effort seriously wounded, the blood
draining from his body, but he demurred at visualizing
the irreparable event, the fatal moment when, losing
consciousness at the same time as his life, he would be
done out of the paean of praise being sung by the *witnesses*. The only way he managed to face this ordeal
was by cheating a little and, in rare moments of ecstasy,
contriving to hear, against all probability, the account
of his fabulous exploits, the list of his posthumous citations, and the murmur of veneration that accompanied
his coffin.

2   Cousin spent the first year of the war in this permanent state of exaltation, and no incident occurred to lessen it. His material self seemed to glide unchecked along the course his ambitious mind had plotted. On being called up, he at once asked to be posted to a fighting unit, even though his personal connections might have enabled him to be employed in a less hazardous position. He went even further: during one of his fits of mysticism, when he felt his possibilities capable of indefinite expansion, he requested and obtained the command of a group of volunteers specializing in hazardous raids. He filled this post for several months, earning the praise and official recognition of his superiors.

As a matter of fact, by some strange feeling of consideration, fate seemed to spare him the rather more harrowing aspects of violence. Many dangerous missions for which he had volunteered were canceled at the last moment by higher authority. He never failed to show his disappointment quite plainly, and thereby retained all the credit for his zeal. The few nocturnal operations he led came off without a hitch. On two or three occasions, when a shot was sent in the direction of his platoon, there were always enough men around him to prevent his feeling that he himself was the target. The knowledge that his men had their eyes fixed on him, together with the vague feeling that the bullets were not actually *seeking him out,* endowed him with the reflexes of a brave man. He had never experienced hand-to-hand fighting.

The debacle of 1940 did nothing to sully the character of the hero who inhabited his mind. His body withstood the ordeal of the large-scale raids, and his conduct at that time earned him further marks of respect. In connection with this attitude of his, Dr. Fog, who later went through every word of his personal file, remarked in parentheses that during a raid on a big town, almost all the inhabitants kept their heads and gave proof of their courage. He added that this clearly argued a peculiar sense of human solidarity in conjunction with a subconscious belief in the law of averages: every individual was convinced that the bombs were far more likely to fall on someone other than himself. But Dr. Fog's critical acumen frequently expressed itself in cynical and sometimes unjustifiable observations.

The order to withdraw, one of the last he was to receive, reached Cousin before the enemy launched its final offensive. He obeyed without delay, like a well-disciplined officer, but not before voicing his indignation at the disgrace of such a retreat.

The withdrawal took him far toward the west along the main roads of France. To begin with, his unit remained intact and he did his best to follow the sporadic and contradictory orders he was given. Then he found himself cut off and out of touch with headquarters, having gradually lost all his men and become attached to a group of deserters and refugees. But he was still convinced that this position had been forced on him against his will by a pusillanimous High Command.

This long journey, carried out for the most part on foot, actually enabled him to enrich his mind with fresh visions and add a little more to his laurels. While his body toiled along in the midst of the crowd, his mind was busy weaving new dreams about the unusual turn that events had taken. Quite clearly, he imagined himself stopping suddenly in the middle of the road and facing the mob. A hero raised by Providence to put an end to their weakness and despair, he then cried out with the cool resolution born of a daring decision:

"Halt! This is where we shall check their advance."

There was a certain amount of opposition. Before facing the enemy, he first had to deal with his own side. He set to work, without any feeling of hate for the stragglers but with the firm determination necessitated by the grave situation. Some of them tried to force their way past him. He then whipped out his revolver —intoxicated by this picture, he even went so far as to reach for his holster and rehearse the gesture—and ordered them back. When this threat proved insufficient, he forthwith shot one or two of the wretches. A solemn silence ensued, but the crowd, realizing at last the feelings that had prompted his action, came to a halt and put themselves under his orders. A nucleus of resistance had been created. It gradually spread to all the other groups wandering aimlessly about the countryside and extended along the highroads until it formed a solid unbroken line, which, under his command and after a series of noteworthy engagements, turned defeat into a striking victory.

This mental vision of his had such an obsessive quality that he became quite oblivious of his plight and lost all sense of time and place. It was thus that he found himself one day in Brittany, having inadvertently followed a column that had diverged from the main stream of the exodus.

Reluctantly emerging from his dream, he peered about him. He noticed he was looked at askance by every group that passed him on the road, and it was not long before he realized why—he had a sort of sixth sense by which he could tell in a flash what others thought about him: he was the only person in uniform. The civilians must have believed he had turned tail in the face of the enemy.

The revelation of this insulting suspicion made the blood rush to his head. He almost let loose at an old man perched on top of a cart who was looking him up and down with an expression of contempt. He was itching to explain himself, to make the fellow understand that he wasn't the sort of man to slink away, and that he only happened to be there because of the orders he had been given. But the cart had already gone past. He shrugged his shoulders and moved on, drawing himself up to his full height and deliberately assuming a soldierly bearing. It was then he saw Morvan in front of him, getting to his feet again after a moment's rest by the side of the road.

Like Cousin, Morvan was in uniform, and Cousin found himself frowning at the sight of him. On his own, and in a filthy, ragged state, this corporal—Cousin had noticed the man's rank—was in all probability a deserter. Perhaps he was one of those soldiers he had seen throwing down their arms and stealing away under cover of the mob. While Cousin was trying to make up his mind about the man, Morvan turned around, caught sight of Cousin, and came back toward him. He was dressed sloppily and had not shaved for several days. His cheeks were hollow and his eyes betrayed apprehension. Cousin did not like his looks at all.

"Sir!" said Morvan.

"Yes?"

He reported in correctly: Corporal Morvan, of a Signal Corps unit. Cousin asked him sternly what he was doing there. Morvan told him what had happened, somewhat diffidently, but to the best of his ability in his evident anxiety to make himself quite clear. He and his unit had been overrun and taken prisoner when they thought they were miles away from the front. But since the Germans who had captured them—a motorized unit thrusting inland—had no time to deal with them, they had simply seized their weapons and destroyed their vehicles; then they had driven on, announcing that the war would soon be over and ordering them to remain where they were.

Morvan had come to the conclusion that anything was better than just staying there until the main body of the enemy troops arrived. He had convinced some of his comrades, Bretons like himself, and they had struck out toward the west without meeting any opposition. He had lost his companions on the way and pushed on alone, marching instinctively in the direction of his village, situated near the Rance, between Dinan and Dinard, which seemed to him the only desirable refuge in these circumstances beyond his comprehension.

Had he done wrong? He questioned Cousin with eyes full of uncertainty. At the start of his trek he had come across a few officers on their own, but none of them had been able to give him definite instructions. He had approached the police, with equal lack of success. A police sergeant had told him, however, that the war was over, or almost, and probably the best thing for everyone was simply to go home. He had therefore kept going. He was now about twenty kilometers away from his village, where his mother must be worrying about him. His one thought at the moment, it was plain, was to lengthen his stride and put her mind at ease as soon as possible.

"Was that the right thing to do, sir?" he asked in an apprehensive tone of voice.

Cousin was appalled by the man's irresolute attitude toward the situation. His own position struck him as being utterly different from Morvan's. Yet, after thinking it over, he had to admit that the extent of the disaster and the general disorganization was some excuse for the mental confusion of certain feeble characters—this corporal, he now felt sure, was lacking in moral fiber—and he made a noncommittal reply in a condescending tone of voice. He told him he was probably not to blame if he had really done all he could to rejoin a fighting unit. Perhaps there would be further orders for him after he got home.

Automatically they went on walking together. Morvan was thankful to have an officer with him. As for Cousin, if he was mortified by the thought that his presence beside Morvan could authorize this runaway to establish an analogy between their respective conducts, he nevertheless saw a certain advantage in his company: two men already formed the nucleus of a platoon and offered less ground for the suspicion of desertion that he had noticed in the eyes of some of the civilians and that still made him smart with shame.

3   "Are you tired, sir?"

Cousin frowned. In this considerate question he thought he detected a tendency to familiarity, which he could not stand in a man like Morvan. However, he really was worn out, having marched for several weeks with scarcely any rest.

"It's nothing," he said, squaring his shoulders with an effort. "It's my duty to keep going."

Although they had barely exchanged a word since joining forces, he had thought it advisable to intimate to his companion that he was engaged on an important secret mission, his purpose being to make it impossible for the corporal to draw a comparison between their respective positions—a fear that had nagged him ever since their meeting. He had given no details—the corporal did not ask for any—but had simply made some vague allusions to certain contacts he had to make, which amounted to half believing in them himself.

"Sir," Morvan went on diffidently, "this is the turn-off to my village. It's less than an hour away. It will soon be dark. I suggest you come and stay the night with us. There's only my mother, who runs a grocery, and my sister. We could put you up if you're not too fussy."

Since Cousin did not reply, he went on in a round-about way to explain at great length that his sister had left school and in normal circumstances worked as a stenographer in the town. But the firm that employed her had shut down at the beginning of the war and she had come back to the village until she could find some other job. Cousin listened to him without paying much attention, concentrating only on his suggestion.

"It'll certainly be better than sleeping out on the roadside, sir," the corporal went on. "Besides, if the Germans come through here, you're liable to be taken prisoner."

"I *must* not be captured," said Cousin.

He had already decided to accept the invitation, and the threat of Germans made his acquiescence seem perfectly natural. He repeated with fierce insistence that, whatever happened, he could not risk falling into enemy hands, as though his personal liberty were a matter of national importance.

"You'll be all right with us. The village is well off the main road."

After hesitating a moment longer, Cousin finally accepted. Morvan was delighted. He seemed desperate not to lose this officer who had miraculously turned up on the road to take the place of all the other missing authorities. Cousin thought with animosity that he had been invited only because his presence would help blind the corporal's family to his somewhat inglorious homecoming.

They walked on through a wooded area where the only sign of human habitation was a handful of scattered cottages buried among the trees. Morvan informed his companion that they were now in the valley of the Rance, not very far from the sea. Presently they reached a village that seemed to be deserted. The inhabitants must have locked up for the night. The grocery was closed. Morvan banged several times on the shutters and called out his name. A moment later Cousin found himself in the presence of Morvan's mother, an old peasant woman with a wrinkled face, and of Claire, his sister, a girl of about twenty, whom he judged at first glance to be made of sterner stuff than her brother.

After being warmly embraced by the two women, Morvan respectfully introduced his companion as an officer on a special mission. Cousin could not help feeling grateful for this and did not contradict him. The idea that he was not simply running away—this idea had so possessed him that it had lost every trace of fiction.

The homely atmosphere dispelled the dreams of valor that had occupied his mind for several days, and at last he thought of asking for news of the war. He had paid little attention to the rumors that were rife on the roads. The two women, who listened to the radio regularly, were aware of the latest developments.

The situation could not be worse. The Germans were everywhere. There was talk of an armistice.

It was Claire who told him this. The old woman merely nodded her head and occasionally muttered the word *"Boche"* with a snarl. Both of them looked utterly dejected, but a gleam came into the girl's eyes when she mentioned the broadcast they had heard the day before. She had not understood it all—the reception had been bad—but she had caught the gist of it. A French general in London had declared that the disaster was not irreparable and had called on his compatriots to come and join him in continuing the struggle.

When she had finished speaking, Cousin noticed that she was gazing at them both, at her brother as well as at him, with a sort of impatience, as though she were waiting for some reaction on their part. He flushed. He felt he ought to answer her unvoiced question. He was about to do so automatically, in the favorable way his deep concern for the opinion of others demanded and also for his own self-respect, when the young girl abruptly switched the conversation.

"You'd better change into civvies," she said to her brother; "and you, too, Lieutenant. And you must be dying of hunger."

She went off to find them some clothes and prepare a meal. An hour later, Cousin, dressed like a peasant in his Sunday best, sat down to dinner with the family in the back parlor, drooping with fatigue and lulled by the peace and quiet of this country retreat. Outside, the village lay wrapped in silence. Claire had switched on the radio and kept glancing at the clock with impatience. The BBC eventually came on the air and they gathered around to listen. It was a rebroadcast of the French general's appeal.

In a flash Cousin felt wide awake, and the gift of intellectual zeal that had been bestowed on him at birth found itself once again roused to its highest pitch. It seemed to him that this appeal was addressed to him alone and that it was the natural justification of his odyssey across France. His exalted imagination established an immediate connection between the program outlined in the broadcast and the mysterious mission on which he had claimed to be engaged. He did not think of the urgent acts implied by his acquiescence. He felt subconsciously that this was a unique enterprise worthy only of a small elite, and the ecstasy into which he was plunged by this idea excluded every other material preoccupation from his mind.

He noticed that Claire was again watching them, Morvan and himself, with the same intent expression she had worn before dinner.

"Some fellows managed to get away yesterday," she said. "They found a trawler. I helped them."

"Get away where?" her brother muttered in amazement.

Morvan, like the others, had listened in silence, but he seemed to have taken in nothing and showed no sign of emotion. Cousin was shocked by this attitude, as though it were a mark of cowardice, and he fancied this lack of enthusiasm was equally galling to Claire. The indignant tone in which he replied reflected his feelings.

"Where? To England, of course! To carry on with the struggle."

"I see," Morvan replied simply, after a moment's reflection. "Do you really think we ought to try and get away, sir?"

"There's no question about it," Cousin said with determination, although he had not yet even considered the practicability of such an enterprise.

"To England?"

"To England."

"If that's the way it is, sir . . ."

Morvan's placid attitude remained unchanged. He was spared all mental confusion by the directives given in such a decisive manner by higher authority. He thought it over for a moment longer, then turned to his sister.

"Where can we find a boat?"

The spontaneity of her reply showed that she had already anticipated this question.

"There are no more transports, but we've still got our little launch. Mother and I managed to hide it away in a creek up the estuary."

Cousin quickly switched his gaze to the old woman, who was taking no part in the conversation and seemed to be lost in her own thoughts.

"What about fuel?" Morvan asked as calmly as before.

"I filled her up, just in case. And there are some spare tins Mother has hidden away."

"In that case, sir . . ." said Morvan. "It's a fine night. I'm not a bad seaman. We shan't be able to get as far as England in the launch, but there's a chance we might be picked up by some Allied vessel out at sea. What should we take with us?"

He was a creature devoid of all imagination. Pure thought was alien to him, and he avoided ideas that were too complicated by reducing them to a practical level. His sister cast a glance of relief in his direction.

Cousin hesitated for a moment, taken unawares both by the suddenness and the simplicity of this decision, resenting the haste that tended to disturb the elements of his dream. He felt it was almost an act of barbarity to let enthusiasm be swamped in this manner by immediate action. He liked to turn heroic projects over in his mind and savor them at greater length. However, he felt he ought to appear even more impulsive than Morvan, and so declared:

"We'll leave just as we are. We don't need anything."

"I've already packed some supplies," said Claire. "There's enough for three people. I'm coming with you."

To her brother's astonishment, she explained that some men from a neighboring village, who had come home a few days earlier, had told her that Morvan had escaped. She and her mother had therefore expected him to turn up sooner or later.

"We got everything ready, just in case," she concluded.

"Good work," said Morvan.

Her completely natural tone and absence of unnecessary remarks elicited in Cousin a mixture of envy and irritation. Her attitude seemed to belittle the heroism of his own conduct. She repeated calmly, "I'm coming with you," and her mother raised no objection. "Just in case," as she put it, everything had been made ready, and there was no use turning back now. Once again he felt that his role demanded a little overacting.

"Let's be off at once," he said, rising to his feet. "We've wasted enough time as it is."

Claire quietly told him that the boat was only an hour away and that they would have to wait a little longer for a favorable tide.

"We'd do better to wait by the boat."

He urged them to hurry. The old woman, in spite of her fortitude, was in tears. Yet she did not try to hold her children back. She realized the danger of the expedition but preferred them to be well out of the way of the Germans, whose imminent arrival filled her with horror.

"You youngsters," she muttered; "it's best for you not to stay here."

Cousin stood in the background, keeping a watchful eye on this farewell scene. Claire was weeping. Morvan had turned his head aside. So they were showing a few signs of weakness at last! This gave him a sense of relief. He would now be able to resume his role of leader. He was familiar with every aspect of it and was glad to know he could play it to perfection. In fact, he played it so well that he succeeded, by his facial expression alone, in convincing the others that it was only from a sense of duty that he was hurrying them on, and that in spite of his commanding, even obdurate, attitude, he himself was having to make an effort to hold back his tears. They were deeply grateful to him for this. When the desired effect had been obtained, his features hardened, and from then on he appeared to them only as the leader who had no right to let his feelings get the better of him. He snatched them from their mother's arms, ordered them to get moving, and hustled them outside, toward the great adventure, without having any feeling that he was being led by them.

With him, mental reactions invariably preceded the physical, but thus far his body had never lagged far behind. It always followed—after a certain lapse of time, to be sure—but it always did follow, urged on by the imperative demands created by his mind.

4   Morvan was not boasting when he said he was a fairly good seaman. Moreover, fortune favored them. They moved out of the estuary, sailed safely through the night, and at first light, having run out of fuel, were sighted by a British patrol vessel that took them on board. The captain had explicit orders concerning seafarers of this sort. He took them straight to a beach in England where a camp for French refugees had been established. There they went through the procedure common to all foreigners arriving by unusual means. They were subjected to several interrogations, sometimes with suspicion but always with courtesy, and over and over again had to answer the question that exasperated a great many men of good will at this period:

"What brought you here?"

They were housed in a tent and informed that they

could not be sent to London for several days. Meanwhile a security officer asked them to prepare as detailed a report as possible on their voyage and to give any information they were in a position to provide. Morvan and his sister handed in their contribution that very evening. It consisted of a single sheet of paper, and the corporal had had to cudgel his brains to expand it even to this length.

Cousin, on the other hand, embarked on this report with the respect that any form of writing inspired in him and with the particular enthusiasm he felt for a series of events in which he had played a leading part. This extraordinary odyssey—it was he who had lived through it, none other than he. He let this idea sink in until it was firmly fixed in his mind, and he felt a thrill of delight at the thought that he had now become, beyond all doubt, a seasoned adventurer.

His opus occupied him all the time they were in camp, which was over a week, yet he did not feel the slightest impatience at the slowness of the administrative machinery that was retarding the realization of his dreams of glory. He needed this breathing space to tot up the score of his exploits, to work out the sum total of his prowess, while setting it off to the best advantage in his own particular medium.

As in all his literary work, he subjected himself to the strictest objectivity and accuracy in dealing with the facts. Facts are intangible, and his talent came into play only with their presentation, their coordination, and the subsequent inquiry into their significance. But even then he was careful not to let himself be carried away by his inspiration. He was held in check by the soundest professional conscience and never allowed a statement to pass without first submitting it to a rigorous critical analysis.

Referring to his meeting with Morvan, for instance, he mentioned, without undue emphasis and with great reserve, that he had been sorry to find him resigned to defeat. This was strictly accurate. Before committing it to paper, he recalled the indignation he had felt when he saw that Morvan's one and only idea was to get back to his village. He added that perhaps there was some excuse for the corporal's momentary lack of resolution and that Morvan had realized where his real duty lay as soon as he, Cousin, had pointed it out. He was sure Morvan would turn out to be a first-rate soldier now that he had been set once again on the right course . . . "and provided he is properly led," he added after a moment's reflection, in an effort to condense his whole opinion into one brief sentence.

In connection with this "duty," which, with supreme tact, he refrained from defining, merely allowing its nature to be implicitly and plainly inferred, a slight confusion of dates had conveniently taken root in his mind. Thus his fierce desire to continue the struggle had inspired every move he had made—in particular his retreat—ever since he had been aware of the disorganization of the army. His decision had been made long before the appeal he had heard on the radio, which had merely served to give a definite material form to his hopes and to a plan he had worked out some time before. It was an insignificant distinction in itself and lent itself quite naturally to his pen, seeing that it gave such a logical and coherent aspect to the memory of his trek.

He did not forget to mention Claire in this document, which he wished to make as complete as possible. After reflecting on her character at great length, he summed up her conduct in a single sentence, in much the same manner he had once used to round off an essay on a particularly difficult subject. He declared that ". . . she must certainly be an extremely plucky girl to have undertaken an expedition that would have daunted many men." Here, too, one must admit, his report adhered strictly to the truth; no one in the world could deny that Claire was a plucky girl. He read this passage over several times and found it met with his entire satisfaction.

They left for London, hoping that the formalities were at last over and done with. There they were put in touch with another service, which handled all French nationals who declared their intention of continuing the struggle on the side of the Allies. The majority were immediately steered into the embryonic staff offices of Free France. A few others, who seemed to be more promising material, were offered the chance of working directly with the British and were given to understand that their talents would be put to use more quickly.

So it happened in this case. Morvan was valuable as a radio operator. Claire was an excellent stenographer, and the Powers That Be know exactly how valuable a good stenographer is in time of war. She spoke English and could also work a radio transmitter, having been initiated into this mystery by her brother. As for Cousin, his degree of education, his officer status, and his brilliant military record singled him out as absolutely first-rate material.

When the offer was put to him, accompanied by a number of laudatory comments on his bearing and conduct, Cousin realized that it applied only to a select few, and did not hesitate for a moment. He accepted immediately and urged his companions to do likewise. They were then allotted quarters in a requisitioned hotel in London and were asked to wait until further notice.

Claire was the first to be summoned, the very next day. The Anglo-French service that was then being hastily organized was in urgent need of stenographers. A few days later Morvan was sent to a camp for training in the latest radio equipment. For Cousin, the period of waiting lasted several weeks; he seemed to have been forgotten. At first he simply felt slightly annoyed; then he launched into a frenzied tirade against English bureaucracy, which, as far as he could see, had no more to recommend it than did that of his own country. He sent the authorities several reminders of his presence, in which his impatience and eagerness for action were expressed in no uncertain terms, and begged to be employed on any dangerous mission.

His patriotism and perseverance were finally rewarded, and the manner in which he was summoned was particularly pleasing to his sense of romance. He received a brief note ordering him to report to London, and eventually found himself facing a strange civilian in what looked like an ordinary business office. He felt a sudden shiver of excitement on discovering, from the ensuing conversation, that he was being invited to work for a service whose name alone conjured up an image of mystery and adventure.

5   The instant he realized he was being asked to take part in clandestine warfare was one of the most sublime moments of his life. His whole body quivered, infused with the breath of the solemn poetry engendered by the thought of special services in wartime, and his dreams at once assumed a new form. Mystery and intrigue added a special pungency to the scent of glory that his mind was forever distilling. A phrase he had once noticed in the course of his reading began buzzing through his brain: "Intelligence work is a noble profession—an occupation for gentlemen."

Before the civilian had even mentioned it, he foresaw the nature of the mission on which he was to be engaged: they were going to send him into France secretly. He had every reason for drawing this conclusion. On several occasions, during his interviews with the authorities, the importance attached to underground activity in enemy-occupied territory had been hinted at in guarded terms. He had often played with the idea of being employed in this field, but it had seemed too wonderful for him to dare to think about. Suddenly realizing he had been far too modest and that he was considered worthy of such a perilous task, he was dazzled by the thought of the possibilities this new universe opened to a man of his mettle.

"I've a certain amount of information about you," the civilian was saying. "At the front, always volunteered for the tough jobs. Fine. I've also read the account of your escape from France. I must congratulate you . . ."

Cousin did not reply, realizing that nothing he could say would add to his reputation, which emerged from the facts alone.

"Again, in London, I see, you applied for a dangerous mission. I've got a particularly tricky one to offer you, more hazardous and worthwhile than anything you're likely to come across in the regular army . . . because, as you're no doubt aware, this means joining a very special service."

An expression of ecstasy came into Cousin's eyes. There was no doubt about it: this civilian, this slightly pot-bellied, middle-aged man with the deceptively casual manner, this ordinary-looking office of his—all this meant not only a secret service, but the world-famous, one and only Intelligence Service. He felt a twinge of condescending pity for some of his compatriots he had met in London who were attempting, with such meager means, to establish an intelligence branch within the framework of Free France. He, Cousin, would be working for the Big Shots, the Kings of the Profession!

"What we need," continued the middle-aged man,

who on occasion was not averse to dilating on the philosophical aspect of his job, "what we need are men of action, certainly—but, above all, we need brains. The ideal agent is someone who possesses a will of iron subordinated to intellectual faculties of the highest order. Lawrence will probably always be the perfect example of this. We believe that you have unique qualifications."

For him, this was tantamount to a revelation. Did he not possess this rare mixture of contradictory qualities? Why hadn't they thought of employing him in this field before? Why hadn't he thought of it himself? He felt almost physically sick as he recalled the commonplace tasks to which he had been restricted in the regular army. As a matter of fact, it now occurred to him that he had always suspected he was destined for greater exploits.

He listened in a daze and with eager impatience while the civilian described his eventual mission in broad outline. He would be sent into France with a radio operator. There he would have to create an intelligence network. So far there was no proper organization. He would be given a free hand and would have to make important decisions on his own initiative.

"We've got any amount of potential material over there, but what we're short of are organizers, you understand?"

Each word was a stimulant to Cousin's pride, and not for a second did he envisage the dangers of this operation. For the moment there was only one clearly defined thought in his head: a strange urge to break off this conversation so as to be able to commune with himself.

He longed to be by himself because the other man's presence hindered the full development of the dreams that were gradually taking shape in his mind. He pictured himself vaguely in the guise of a mysterious X, an unknown figure but famous throughout France because of his exploits, a phantom warrior who, during the still watches of the night, was discussed in excited whispers in the towns and in the countryside, who escaped every trap the enemy set, thanks to his superhuman cunning, and who emerged from the shadows only on the day of victory. His mind had an imperative need of solitude to put these fleeting images in order and to find the ideal form for their incarnation by drawing on a mass of material details that could be brought to light only in peaceful seclusion.

He accepted the offer without questioning a single point and declared himself ready to start as soon as they wished. The civilian seemed pleased with this impetuosity but informed him that first of all he would have to go through a special training course.

Before even embarking on this stage, he would have to report to several offices and submit to a rigorous cross-examination carried out by a number of experts. He acquiesced to these formalities without showing too much impatience.

One of these specialists, who interrogated him in French, first asked him a number of questions that seemed to have no bearing at all on his new functions, before concentrating on his past activities, his antecedents, and the state of his health. Cousin felt it was like being put through a medical examination of a rather special kind. The examiner actually was a doctor; in fact, he was a psychiatrist—Dr. Fog.

After the interrogation, which Cousin thought perfectly absurd, Dr. Fog switched without a pause to his mission and asked him when he was thinking of starting.

"As soon as possible," Cousin declared. "If it depended on me alone, I'd be off tonight."

Dr. Fog scrutinized him with his inquisitorial eyes, and a vague look of disappointment crept into his expression. He made no comment, however.

"Really?" he merely remarked noncommittally.

Cousin felt that he had somehow made a bad mistake. That special sense of his, which enabled him to follow the variations of other people's opinion of himself, warned him that his reply, which would have satisfied most authorities, was not to the liking of this new individual. He corrected himself, assuming a more subdued tone of voice.

"That is to say, as soon as I've finished the training course."

"I thought as much," the doctor muttered. He paused for a moment, then went on, observing Cousin closely again. "I suppose you realize the dangers to which you're likely to be exposed?"

"I'm fully aware of them."

Dr. Fog nevertheless insisted on enlarging on the subject. He did so in no uncertain terms and with a wealth of detail that argued extensive knowledge, if not personal experience. For a quarter of an hour he described the various methods employed by the enemy to make an Allied secret agent talk: from plain blows, cunningly administered so as to dull the brain, to the most atrocious tortures, including the water treatment and electric shocks.

Cousin showed a reasonably bold front as he listened to this long list of atrocities. He had never been frightened by words, and these particular ones did not really faze him. Nevertheless, he had to make an effort to withstand the doctor's piercing gaze right up to the end and, when he had finished, to answer him in measured tones.

"I'm fully aware of all that and I'm prepared to face those dangers."

"Would you also be prepared to swallow this, if necessary?" said Dr. Fog, opening a small cardboard box.

"What is it?"

"Cyanide. For use in special services, it exists in different forms—pills or capsules. I recommend these tiny glass capsules. If you manage to slip one into your mouth without being noticed, you can keep it under your tongue until you feel the point has come when you can't stand the pain any longer. I know it's singularly difficult to tell exactly when this crucial moment has been reached," Dr. Fog observed parenthetically, "but if you are very tough and don't lose your head, you still have a chance right up to the very end. If you feel you're coming to the end of your strength and are about to talk, to betray, then a simple snap of the teeth, and it's all over. . . . I hope you will have no occasion to use it, but it's an eventuality for which all good agents must be prepared."

Dr. Fog attached a great deal of importance to this

sort of test and made it compulsory for certain candidates. He maintained that their reactions gave him a valuable clue to their character. Cousin had turned pale; he stiffened in his seat for a moment, as though hypnotized by the small glass phial, but quickly pulled himself together. The doctor, who was watching him closely, detected no more than a slight tremor in his hand when he took the capsule and an almost imperceptible quaver in his voice as he replied:

"I won't forget your instructions, sir. I, too, hope that I shan't have to resort to this solution, but in case I do I'll try to make sure when the right moment arrives."

He had even succeeded in introducing a note of irony into his voice. He fancied his examiner appreciated this, and felt well rewarded for the effort.

"Don't leave that lying about for anyone to pick up," said the doctor as he dismissed him.

Dr. Fog, however, did not appear to be completely satisfied. He nervously thumbed through a file that lay before him, nodding his head, reread some notes he himself had scribbled down, then thrust the papers into a drawer and sat back lost in thought. His meditation was interrupted by the entry of the middle-aged man who had interviewed Cousin when he first reported. He had heard the whole conversation from the adjacent office, the door having been left ajar. He knew the doctor well and was aware that he did not like to be hurried. He sat down quietly opposite him, lit a cigarette, and after a minute's pause observed:

"A good candidate, I think."

Dr. Fog did not reply.

"Nevertheless," the middle-aged man went on, as though he had been contradicted, "he's got a first-class record."

Dr. Fog still did not utter a word.

"I noticed," the other man continued patiently, "that you spoke to him in a particularly harsh manner."

"Really?"

"One would have thought you wanted to discourage him about the job."

"A noble profession," Dr. Fog muttered blandly.

"Do you see anything against employing him?"

"As far as special services are concerned," said Dr. Fog, without answering the question directly, "the Nazi methods have at least one advantage over ours. They don't stop at theoretical experiments. They test their agents' capacity of resistance properly, in an extremely realistic way."

"That couldn't happen over here."

"I know."

"Well, what's your verdict?"

"An intellectual," the doctor replied hesitantly, "an intellectual. You never know where you are with that sort. They may be capable of sublime sacrifices or else break down at the very first crisis, and then that's the end of them. I'll have to think it over at greater length."

"We haven't the time."

"Then take him on," the doctor retorted rather testily. "After all, from my point of view, I see no serious objection."

"Is he normal mentally?"

"Normal?" The psychiatrist gave a shrug of impatience and the middle-aged man got up to leave. "First you'll have to define the norm. All I can say is, I've known crazier people than him in the service . . . even in the higher ranks," Dr. Fog concluded as his visitor left the room.

6   The Gestapo raid on the Lachaume farm brought an end to a series of brilliant successes and to the luck that had favored him since the beginning of the war, particularly during the first few months of his new activities. He felt as though a brutal stroke of an ax had descended upon him. Not only was he paralyzed in every limb, but almost all his vital functions were suspended, reduced instantaneously to a thunderous beat of his heart and to a dull ache that spread throughout his frame as a result of this inhuman hammering.

He was plunged abruptly into a state of absolute passivity, like a patient whose reflexes are deadened by an injection before a serious operation. He made no attempt to get hold of his submachine gun, which was in a cupboard within arm's reach. His brain was incapable of issuing a single order or even of thinking of putting up a fight, and in any case his body would have refused to obey.

Yet he could have fought back. He had been granted a few minutes' grace, thanks to the heroism of old Lachaume, who gave a shout in the yard outside as soon as he spotted the vehicles; but the shout and the shots that ensued, instead of spurring him to action, stupefied him completely. Morvan, who was in the middle of sending off a message, displayed more presence of mind and resourcefulness than Cousin would have given him credit for. His eyes caught those of his officer, begging for the order that Cousin was incapable of giving. Then, since the Germans' footsteps could already be heard on the stairs, Morvan snatched up all the papers that lay scattered on the table and stuffed them into the stove, where they burned to ashes. After that he dashed across to the cupboard where the weapons were kept. He did not have time to reach it. Four men armed with submachine guns burst into the room. Cousin, looking as white as a ghost, had not moved a muscle.

This conduct on the part of Morvan made Cousin feel strangely unhappy during the short respite he was given while the Germans were busy searching the farm. Now that the effect of the shock was wearing off, he had recovered his mental faculties, and the agony of mind he felt at what fate had in store still did not prevent him from regarding his subordinate's behavior as an insult.

Chance had brought them together again, Morvan and himself, for this mission in France. It certainly had not been his choice. He had even raised certain objections when he was told that the corporal had been attached to him as a radio operator. Morvan was clearly lacking in spirit, in drive, and the first requirement for an enterprise of this sort was a thirst for action. Chosen because of his technical skills, he was merely prepared to obey orders and go wherever he was told. Cousin did his utmost to drive this point home with the English staff officer who was responsible for mounting the operation, but the latter refused to see reason.

"You already know each other, since you came over here together."

"But that was pure coincidence. . . . Mind you, I've nothing definite against him. He put on a good show. But I'm not sure he's the right man for this sort of job . . ."

"You'll have to make do with him. We're short of French specialists, and he's a first-class radio operator."

Cousin had acquiesced, with certain reservations. In his dealings with Morvan, while the preparations for their departure were being made, he occasionally felt a violent urge to humiliate him by revealing his contempt. He assumed a haughty, biting tone of voice. He discouraged the friendly relationship that, in special services, was more customary than a hidebound insistence on discipline. With a heavily patronizing air, he would say something of this sort:

"I don't know if they've told you, Morvan, but the smallest detail of this mission is of paramount importance and must be treated as top secret."

"Yes, sir," Morvan would reply.

With his increased responsibilities, Cousin had been promoted to the rank of major, and with due regard for military hierarchy Morvan started calling him *"mon commandant,"* which flattered him but which might prove somewhat risky in France. Cousin pointed this out to Morvan, who thereupon had reverted quite naturally to plain "sir."

"I just wanted to warn you. When we're in enemy-occupied territory, of course, it goes without saying— we've been into that already and I hope you haven't forgotten what you have to do when the time comes— but even here . . ."

Cousin had told him about the cyanide capsules. With a sort of relish he had re-enacted the scene to which he had been subjected in Dr. Fog's office, the roles now being reversed. Playing his part with exaggerated gravity, he watched his colleague's reactions with an almost morbid curiosity. He considered them pretty disappointing and felt even more proud of himself. Morvan, it must be admitted, was badly shaken. Then he pulled himself together. Even though Cousin offered him a loophole, telling him there was still time to back out, that he would not hold it against him— how he longed and prayed for such an admission of weakness!—Morvan finally declared he could stick it out as well as the next man and that he was ready to leave, since he had been selected.

". . . Even here in London, don't forget that walls have ears and that any loose talk, no matter how insignificant it may seem, could lead to disaster . . ."

"I know that, sir. I'll hold my tongue all right."

"Have you got a girl friend here?" Cousin went on, looking him straight in the eye.

"No, sir," Morvan replied, blushing scarlet.

"Good. This business is so important that even if you were married, your wife could not be told what you were up to. Do you understand?"

"Only my sister knows that I'm leaving, but it wasn't I who told her."

"It's not your fault, but it's a pity just the same."

Claire knew about their mission because she now held a fairly important post, as secretary to one of the heads of the service. Cousin, although he was convinced of her discretion, was anything but pleased that she was acquainted with the project and never missed an opportunity to make her brother conscious of this.

The Germans went on with their search and appeared not to bother about the two men. After feverishly racking his brains, Cousin came to the conclusion that there was nothing incriminating for them to find —except the radio set, of course! Even in his suitcase there was no document that could betray their activities. The only dangerous papers were the ones Morvan had burned.

Morvan had shown great presence of mind, admittedly. Quick reactions—Cousin was forced to recognize this, albeit reluctantly. But then, think of the ingenuity he himself had displayed in the six months he had been operating as a spy under the very nose of the enemy!

After looking into several enterprising schemes involving a submarine landing or a parachute drop, he had returned to France quite openly, with Morvan, in broad daylight and under his own name, crossing over from Spain with a group of his compatriots who had opted for the Vichy regime and were allowed to leave England. He played his part so well that he allayed all suspicion. He managed to pass himself off as a fervent supporter of collaboration, which made it easier for him to travel about the country and embark on his undercover intelligence activities. He established valuable contacts in several districts and gradually built up a network that provided a considerable amount of information. Living for the most part in the Free Zone, he succeeded in extending his organization into Occupied France. He had found an ideal infiltration point, the Lachaume farm, a tumble-down building just south of the border, whose owner, a rather simple-minded old man, lived alone and had agreed to put the place at his disposal for a modest remuneration. A born poacher, Lachaume knew every inch of the surrounding countryside, and crossing the line was child's play to him. Cousin often used the farm as a meeting place for agents arriving from the north.

He chided himself for having made his visits there too long and too frequent, but the place suited him perfectly. Its peaceful atmosphere and isolated situation were conducive to the vast schemes he kept turning over in his mind. On this occasion he had been there for over a week, having made it his headquarters for various operations—in particular, for an important raid that was to take place that very evening, in a few hours' time, about thirty miles away: the sabotage of a railroad roundhouse.

He had planned the whole thing with infinite care, attending to every detail himself. It was the first time he had organized an operation of this kind. As he had been told in the course of his training, action groups, and those responsible for intelligence, should always restrict themselves to their own specific functions, and he belonged to the latter. But considering the cooperation he had managed to obtain in this district, the opportunity seemed so perfect that London finally gave its approval to the scheme, forbidding him, however, to take part in the actual raid, as he was too valuable to risk. He had acquiesced with great reluctance, inveighing against the hidebound attitude of the bureaucrats who deprived him of this fun. The leader of the raiding party was to send him a runner on the following day to inform him of the result, which Morvan would then wire back from the farmhouse.

Morvan had been with him ever since his return to France. He had acquitted himself well; there was no denying it. Cousin even admitted objectively that he was a useful colleague and that his initial distrust seemed groundless. Morvan was obviously discreet and knew his job backward. Thanks to him, contact with London was maintained permanently, and he had succeeded in recruiting and training other operators in various parts of the country.

Cousin had not seen fit to conceal his satisfaction. Little by little he had abandoned his stand-offish attitude. He had even gone so far as to acquaint Morvan with a number of the network's secrets and the names of several important agents. Morvan therefore knew all about the operation that had been planned for that night.

Cousin now cursed himself for having been so indulgent. How could he tell if Morvan, without any intention of doing mischief, but by letting slip some thoughtless remark, was not responsible for the disaster? Someone had talked, that was obvious. The dislike he had instinctively felt for Morvan at the start welled up all over again.

He was just beginning to convince himself that Morvan was at the root of the trouble when the Gestapo leader came over toward him with a deliberately casual air that sent a shiver down his spine.

7   The Germans had found nothing, but a mere glance at their officer's face made Cousin realize they were not going to relinquish their prey. They must have been well informed to have made straight for the farmhouse. If they had accorded the Frenchmen a few minutes' respite and had appeared not to bother about them, apart from slipping handcuffs around their wrists, this was not due to hesitation on their part. It was part of their usual procedure to punctuate brutal treatment with intervals of inactivity that gave the victim fresh grounds for hope, so as to crush his spirit all the more thoroughly with a subsequent spell of violence.

The officer's expression now indicated that the serious business was about to begin. He spoke French fairly well. He turned to Cousin.

"Mr. Cousin?"

Too terrified to speak, Cousin gave a nod of assent.

"I've known about you for some time, Mr. Cousin. I've suspected your activities for several months, but I wanted to catch you red-handed. I must congratulate you. You've been pretty clever up to now. I was beginning to think I might even have been mistaken about you."

In spite of his mental anguish, Cousin felt a surge of childish pride at the thought of his merits being recognized by the enemy; but this petty satisfaction was soon destroyed.

"But this seems to me conclusive proof of your activities," the Gestapo officer went on in an icy tone, indicating the radio transmitter. "I feel sure you won't make any difficulty about giving me all the information I want on your work and your accomplices. There are several questions I should like to ask you, and this will do to begin with: What have you been doing in this place for over a week?"

Cousin did not reply. His mental turmoil was such that he could not think of a single excuse, no matter how improbable. The officer then turned to Morvan and put the same question to him. Morvan, whose face was ashen white, also held his tongue. Cousin sensed that he was trying to catch his eye, but he could not bring himself to raise his head.

"So you're not prepared to answer, is that it?"

The officer stepped back and held a brief consultation in an undertone with one of his colleagues who appeared to be second in command. Cousin, who spoke German fluently, understood from this that they could not decide whether to take the prisoners away at once or to hold a preliminary interrogation on the spot.

The strange emphasis laid on the word "interrogation" made him shudder. His fears increased when he gathered that the officer, after hearing his subordinate's opinion, was in favor of the second procedure.

"Don't forget," the latter reminded him, "that the *Abwehr* are also following this scent, and have been for some time, I know. If we waste any time, they're liable to beat us to it."

"You're right. Anyway, it's best to strike while the iron's hot. They're still under the effects of shock; we mustn't give them time to recover. The equipment we've got here will do quite nicely," the officer added, glancing across at the stove.

He gave some brief instructions to his men. Two of them seized Cousin by the shoulders and dragged him toward the door. Two others took hold of Morvan, removed his shoes and socks, then proceeded to tie him up, while the second-in-command stirred the embers and put some more wood on the fire. Before being hauled off into the adjoining room, Cousin heard Morvan speak for the first time since the tragedy occurred.

"You can rest assured, sir, I won't talk."

Cousin opened his mouth to speak, for he felt it was his duty as an officer to say a word or two of encouragement in reply. His voice was stifled by an alarming sight that paralyzed him all over again—one of the brutes had smashed his clenched fist into Morvan's face.

Taking their time, Cousin's guards proceeded to light an old cast-iron stove similar to the one in the next room. Smoke billowed out and presently the flames began to roar. Then, before his eyes, they plunged a poker into the embers and left it there. He was suddenly overwhelmed by the horror of his plight. Until then his mind had refused to countenance it, so monstrous did it appear. Tears of despair welled up at the prospect that now confronted him in all its ghastly reality—he was the one who was going to be tortured.

He was the one . . . An inhuman cry from the adjoining room made his blood run cold and reminded him that he was not alone in this desperate predicament. They had started on Morvan. The screaming lasted several seconds. At first it increased in volume as it rose in pitch, like a sound wave issuing from some infernal region augmented by the united shrieks of all the damned; then it gradually diminished and was succeeded by a sort of rattling gasp, ending up in an almost inaudible whimper.

In spite of himself, Cousin started to form a mental picture of the process of the torture. Its nature was only too clear, and it was childish to try to envisage each of its successive phases; but his mind had to have some sort of intellectual exercise, at the risk of breaking down altogether.

The Gestapo men were in a hurry. They were afraid their inveterate rivals, the *Abwehr,* might cut the grass from under their feet. They had neither the time nor the equipment for their usual methods of refined torture. They seized what chance provided—red-hot iron —and chance had provided one of the vilest atrocities imaginable. Morvan's screams were the result of a glowing poker being applied to the soles of his feet. It was allowed to remain there, against the bare flesh, for a second, or perhaps not even as long as that the first time; then it was removed, giving the victim a respite to enable him to imagine the horror of further contact with it.

How long a respite? Cousin struggled pointlessly to try to estimate the space of time, while the whimpering sounded like a prayer that this pause be continued indefinitely.

A second scream, more horrible than the first, was followed by the same throttled gasp, ending up in the same drawn-out whimper. Morvan was keeping his promise: he was refusing to talk. He had reassured Cousin on that score but had received no word of encouragement in return. Cousin had not dared to reply.

He had not dared because of the blow of the clenched first that had been provoked by this defiant declaration. He was paralyzed, just as he had been when the Gestapo burst in, by the fear of similar punishment, against which his whole body rebelled. It had needed this morning's incidents to open his eyes to the insurmountable repulsion that violence inflicted on him.

The infernal wave of sound punctuating his colleague's torture reverberated through his body once more—for the fourth time. He went on trying to estimate each phase of this monstrous cycle and noticed that the frequency was being gradually accelerated as time went on. The butchers were in a hurry. Was it possible for Morvan to hold out much longer? In some incongruous way this question, which obsessed him, suddenly seemed to offer fresh grounds for hope. At first it was no more than a faint glimmer, onto which his mind fastened with desperate tenacity. He made a superhuman effort not to let it fade away, realizing that for him it represented the miraculous means of salvation that fate sometimes tenders to those it has crushed. Gradually it took a more definite shape, until it became crystal clear. If Morvan talked—he knew almost all the secrets of the network—if he talked . . . ! Cousin realized that for some time, ever since Morvan had been dragged off, his subconscious had been hoping for this miracle to occur. This was a wonderfully tantalizing hypothesis to consider. If Morvan talked, it meant salvation for him, Cousin. His interrogation would serve no purpose. He would save his honor and his own skin at one and the same time.

He found himself listening to his colleague's groans with a passionate interest and mental anguish of a completely different kind. But Morvan had already been branded five times; presently, no doubt, the butchers would get tired of this and turn their attentions to him. The poker that had been earmarked for him was probably red-hot by now.

It was too unfair! Morvan was bound to give in. The Gestapo men must have thought so too, since they had selected him as their first victim. Cousin felt an absurd surge of pride at the thought that they were such expert physiognomists, such astute psychologists. Morvan was the one who was bound to talk, not he. Morvan's lack of moral fiber showed in his uncompromising features. . . . Moreover, hadn't he already indulged in careless talk, and more than once? Wasn't he alone responsible for this disaster? How he, Cousin, regretted having taken the man into his confidence! A leader of his caliber should keep his secrets to himself. For he was a real leader—London had congratulated him on his resourcefulness and courage. Always volunteered for the most dangerous jobs . . . whereas this fellow Morvan, who was about to betray them, who was probably giving everything away at this very moment . . .

Another scream brought him down to earth again. The shock of the vibration was so violent that his body gave a jerk and his jaws almost crushed the tiny glass capsule, Dr. Fog's sinister gift, which he had succeeded in taking out of its hiding place and slipping into his mouth in spite of the handcuffs around his wrists. The two Gestapo men who were attending to the fire looked up at him, then shrugged their shoulders and went on with their work.

The gesture of slipping the capsule into his mouth had been a desperate revival of his failing will, still fiercely trying to delude itself as to its true nature. He knew now—he had known it even at the moment of making the proud gesture—that he would never have the nerve to break the glass. But this parody of heroic determination succeeded in deceiving him; and, above all, this semblance of decisive preparation for the supreme sacrifice impressed the ever-present witnesses to his dreams.

Meanwhile the cold, smooth surface against his tongue inspired him with horror. Deliberately bite through the glass? Out of the question! A new fear had seized him when he had given that involuntary start—supposing, in one of those spasms, he broke the capsule and swallowed the poison by mistake!

The whimpering had stopped and he waited in vain for the beginning of a fresh cycle. Had Morvan talked at last? The door of the room was pushed open and the creaking of its hinges appeared to him as a sinister portent. The Gestapo officer strode in. He looked extremely sullen. Morvan . . . ? Cousin shut his eyes for fear of reading the answer in the other man's expression.

PART TWO

8   It was in Dr. Fog's office that the young medical officer, Lieutenant Austin, heard Cousin's name mentioned for the first time.

He was at the hospital, in the middle of one of his routine visits, when he was handed a message from the military authorities asking him to report that very day to a certain branch of the War Office. Austin was not particularly surprised. After being wounded in France and subsequently posted to London, he had applied for fresh employment in a fighting unit. He assumed this summons was the answer to his request.

He began to feel some surprise only when the colonel who interviewed him asked him point-blank if he was prepared to join an intelligence unit. Austin, who had been bored with administrative duties for some time and longed for something more active, at once greeted this proposal as the fulfillment of his dearest wishes. In all good faith, however, he felt it was his duty to point out that he was merely a doctor and had no particular qualifications for a secret agent's work.

"That's no concern of mine," the colonel replied impatiently. "I don't have much to do with those gentlemen myself, but they're the ones who've singled you out."

"Me? They?"

"One of their V.I.P.'s to whom we humble regular soldiers can refuse nothing, even if he asked for our entire personnel. Do you want the job, yes or no?"

Austin felt he had made enough fuss already and accepted the offer, convinced that there must be some mistake.

"That's settled, then. We can strike you off our roster as from today. Now, off you go and report to this Dr. Fog. Here's the address. You'll be under his auspices from now on."

"Dr. Fog!"

"He's the one who asked for you; he'll tell you all about it himself. Cloak-and-dagger stuff, of course. If anyone asks me, I don't know a thing about you. Off you go now."

Austin saluted and left the room. Before reporting to the address he had been given, he consulted a medical directory and found what he was looking for at once: Dr. Fog, Specialist in Mental Diseases. The name was followed by an impressive string of initials.

His memory had not played him false. It was definitely the same Dr. Fog, a psychiatrist of considerable repute in medical circles, with whom he had been in correspondence shortly before the war. He had just graduated and was eager to specialize in the same branch. He had written to ask for advice and had applied for an interview. The doctor had answered all his questions and fixed an appointment for a rather long time ahead because of a journey he had to make. After his return, war was declared and Austin was sent to France. Since then he had not ventured to renew his request for an interview.

It was Dr. Fog himself who was now asking to be remembered to him—and in what peculiar circumstances! What on earth could he have in common with special services? And how was he, Austin, meant to fit into the picture? He did not worry unduly about this second question. As for the first, it was made clear at the outset of their conversation, as soon as he had been shown into a sumptuous chamber—a room more like a drawing room than an office, with thick carpets on the floor, some massive pieces of furniture, and a sober color scheme relieved by an occasional touch of fantasy. This room, situated in a quiet backwater of London, was used for work, research, contemplation, and various elaborate speculations. It was Dr. Fog's private study.

"I suppose you're wondering what this is all about, Austin. I'll satisfy your curiosity right away. I'm not one for making a mystery of things with my close colleagues. I can have complete confidence in your discretion, I trust?"

Austin assured him he was capable of keeping a secret. The doctor paused for a moment, then went on:

"I know you're a sound sort of chap. Anyway, I've got quite a lot of information about you. . . . Yes, we've been keeping an eye on you, without your knowing it, just for the sake of the old routine. We wanted to make sure that you weren't drunk before six in the evening and didn't sleep with a different girl every night. From my point of view, what matters far more is your training, the plans you have in mind, the branch you want to specialize in, and the letters you wrote me. All that's perfect. So, since you're prepared to work with me . . . You're quite sure about that, are you?"

"Quite sure, sir," Austin replied. He realized he was dealing with a very important person and had never for a moment dreamed of questioning his proposal.

"In that case I want you to have a complete picture of my service. Don't hesitate to ask if there's anything you don't understand. To begin with, as you no doubt realize, I hold a fairly important and very special position in a secret organization."

At such an ingenuous statement, Austin, who had a feeling that his new chief was not so trusting as he led one to believe, found it difficult to suppress a smile. Dr. Fog, whom nothing escaped, changed his tone.

"Yes, I see . . . I was forgetting you were one of us, or almost. You're thinking, 'He's treating me like one of his patients. First rule with mental cases—put them at their ease. All this is part of the bedside manner.' Isn't that true?"

Austin blushed and sketched a vague gesture of denial. It was exactly what he had been thinking. The doctor gave a shrug and went on:

"Anyway, this is roughly what you ought to know. It will spare you from racking your brains about it, and I want your brains to be devoted to something more useful. . . . As I was saying, I work for a branch of the secret service. . . . Does that surprise you? It shouldn't. Personally, I believe the psychiatrist is an indispensable adjunct to national defense in wartime, if only for the purpose of weeding out the dangerous lunatics, both military and civilian, who happen to be in important positions. Don't you agree?"

At the doctor's solemn air, Austin again had to suppress a smile and agreed that specialists in mental diseases had a most important role to play in time of war.

"But I was given to understand, sir, that it was not only as a doctor . . ."

"Don't be so impatient. That's how I started off, at any rate, though it's some time ago. I was beginning to have quite a reputation in scientific circles when one of the pundits of the service took it into his head to call me in to examine an important agent who was going to be dispatched overseas. He was not the sort of man to make a hasty decision, you see. Like all pundits, he always took the advice of competent technicians. For once he had given some thought to intellectual qualifications, which was quite bright of him. I accepted the job. Apparently he was satisfied with the way I handled it, since he subsequently kept coming back to me for further advice. In the end I was given an official position. The new candidates were sent along to me before being definitely engaged. Some of the old ones as well, for the mind cracks up fairly easily in this job. I put them through a series of tests. My diagnosis was meant to answer the following questions: Will he made a good agent? If so, in which branch should he be employed —intelligence, action, counterespionage, or what?"

"A sort of professional orientation, based on scientific data, in a very specialized field, sir?"

"That's about it. I soon developed an intense interest in these duties. There were sometimes some very odd types among those candidates."

The doctor paused for a moment, lost in thought, as he recalled certain cases to mind. Then he went on:

"Yes, very strange fellows indeed, and engaged in very strange business, too. I had to exercise a great deal of tact and caution. A congenital idiot can sometimes do a very useful job in this profession, whereas an infinitely gifted man may make a deplorably bad agent."

The doctor fell silent again, then sharply exclaimed:

"If I had vetoed the employment of every idiot, Austin, I should have more or less drained the service, do you realize that?"

"I can well believe it, sir," Austin replied without batting an eyelid.

"Since the war it has been even more tricky, as there are some missions that could hardly be carried out at all except by complete lunatics. On those occasions our job is to find out in what way a given form of mental derangement can be put to the best use. I tell you, Austin, it's terribly exciting work. I'm sure you'll be absolutely fascinated by it."

He rubbed his hands together with obvious satisfaction. His eyes, which had become intensely expressive, sparkled with delight as he described the rewards of his unusual profession. At that moment, in spite of his affable attitude, in spite of the background of this office, which seemed specially designed to create an atmosphere of confidence and well-being, Austin could not help feeling there was something diabolical about him. He suppressed a momentary shudder, without being able to make up his mind whether this feeling was caused by a certain diffidence regarding the moral aspect of this strange orientation, or by the pleasure of discerning a touch of the unusual in his future duties with Dr. Fog. The latter realized the impression he had created and changed his tone.

"Don't for a moment imagine that our work is necessarily sinister, Austin. There's a very pleasant side to it sometimes."

"Oh, I'm sure," the young man replied politely.

"As, for instance, when the pundit I told you about applied for an interview himself. . . . I put him through all the tests with my usual punctiliousness and with particular care, you may be sure. Would you like to know what the result was?"

"I'd be very interested to hear."

"Unemployable in any capacity. Distinct mental instability. A tendency to paranoia. Unresponsive reflexes. The last man in the world to engage as an agent. I should have opposed his being employed on any mission whatsoever. He took it badly to begin with, but he had to come around in the end—the results of the tests leave no room for ambiguity."

"You actually told him that, sir?"

"He ordered me to tell him."

"What did he do? Resign?"

"Not at all. I pulled certain strings to have him promoted. He's now a bigger pundit than ever and merely directs operations at a very high level. His deficiencies warranted a position of this sort; they even indicated his peculiar suitability for it. It was the only solution. Since then there has been noticeable progress in every branch of the service. There you have a singularly fascinating example of 'professional orientation,' as you call it."

9   Once again Austin had to suppress **a** smile at Dr. Fog's serious demeanor. After a moment's hesitation, he screwed up his courage and said:

"As far as I can see, sir, my work will be mostly theoretical. I was hoping . . ."

"Wait a moment, I haven't finished yet. I, too, have had a . . . a sort of promotion. I still interview certain candidates in this office, but only the most important ones. I no longer deal with the small fry now that my field of activity has been enlarged. This is what I'm leading up to. As you can imagine, this job entails a great deal of specialized work and research on the methods, scope, and types of secret-service missions. I had to have free access to all the files. Close contact with the people at the top was also absolutely essential. At first they wouldn't hear of it. With their mania for mystery and secrecy, they preferred to regard me as one of their numerous specialists who are not allowed to know a thing about general organization—a cipher expert, for instance. They would only give me the information I needed in dribs and drabs. One day I lost my temper and put it to them point-blank: either they let me have what I wanted or else I resigned. It seems they thought sufficiently highly of me to agree. Since then we've worked together far more closely. I'm no longer restricted to laboratory tests. I've been able to follow the agents at every stage of their careers and keep a complete file on them—there's nothing like observing a man in action. I've been kept informed of their successes and also of their failures. I've sometimes watched them operate at extremely close range. To cut a long story short, I've now become . . ."

"A sort of head of personnel?"

"Rather more than that, perhaps," Dr. Fog replied with a smile, which convinced Austin once and for all of his chief's importance. "I'm sometimes asked for advice outside my own field of specialization. I've been also required to make certain decisions."

Under Austin's fascinated gaze, he continued briskly:

"But when I have to act on my own initiative, Austin, the personnel is invariably my main consideration, and particularly the intellect of the personnel. Brains are an essential factor in this profession."

"I'm sure of that, sir."

"So now you realize why I need assistants like you. I've got very few of them. I'm a difficult man to please, but I hope you and I will get along together. You already have some experience with the human brain; that's clear from your letters. You're young and eager to get on, I believe . . ."

"So on the whole, sir," said Austin, who was fascinated at the prospect of the exciting missions for which he might be made responsible, "on the whole, I can look forward to leading a fairly active life."

"I'm glad that's the attitude you take," the doctor replied, rubbing his hands together again. "I can see we understand each other. By the way, I noticed in your file that you speak French fluently?"

"As well as I do English, sir. My mother was French and I was partly brought up abroad."

Thereupon, after giving him a few more general particulars, Dr. Fog informed Austin that his job would be to deal with French affairs and, for a start, with one particular case in which he was deeply interested.

"Let's begin with the essentials. First and foremost, the man in question is an agent. Here's his file. You'll have to go through it with great care. It's a rather tricky case, I think, but I'm relying on your judgment. Tell me what you think of it."

He had lowered his voice and assumed a somewhat solemn tone. Austin sensed there was something mysterious afoot and waited with growing impatience for the rest of the story.

"He's a Frenchman," Dr. Fog continued. "I examined him some time ago. Since then I've been given a great deal more information about him."

He started thumbing through the file, picking out a phrase here and there for Austin's benefit.

"A writer in civilian life, an intellectual . . . On active service always volunteered for the dangerous jobs . . . In principle there's nothing wrong with that . . . One of those heroes who escaped from their own country . . . Nothing wrong with that, either . . . Sent back to France, carried out various clandestine operations with zeal and intelligence . . . Ah, here's the hitch . . . His mission ended in disaster, but it wasn't his fault . . . Managed to escape . . . Well, you can read it all for yourself. When you've finished, we'll put our heads together and see if this chap is still employable and, if so, in which branch. If he is, mind you, there's only one possible solution. He'll have to come directly under me—the others, the professionals in the service, don't trust an agent who has been captured by the enemy, even if he does escape . . . I may as well tell you now, Austin, I've often been known to give people a second chance when they've been turned down by the other sections. So far the results haven't been too bad. . . .

"Well, anyway, this fellow was put out of harm's way . . . Given some trivial staff job or other—perhaps with good reason, who knows? But we're terribly short of people with brains, and he's certainly no fool. That's how I came across him. His name is Cousin. We'll have to think of a new name for him now. Names can be quite important; I usually try to choose one that suggests a particular characteristic of the man in question, often in a very roundabout way. Think it over, will you."

"I will, sir."

"We'll go into it again when you've been through the file."

He rose to his feet. As he reached the door, Austin asked:

"You've already examined him, sir?"

"Very briefly, several months ago."

"Is he a normal case?"

" 'Normal' is a word that doesn't mean very much, you know. His brain seems to function correctly. And yet . . ."

Dr. Fog fell silent for a moment, then a strange look came into his eyes, the same glitter that had suggested something satanic to Austin's mind. He went on with a smile, giving his assistant a friendly tap on the shoulder:

"When you get to know me better, Austin, you'll realize that normal people—I mean absolutely normal in the ordinary sense of the word—don't interest me at all. I don't have any truck with them myself. I send them along to another section."

10   "Well, what's your verdict, Austin?"

These were the words with which Dr. Fog greeted him when he came into the office two days later, just as though he had always belonged to the service. To justify this confidence, Austin decided to give his opinion without further delay. He had spent the whole night working on Cousin's file, which filled him with admiration for the personality that emerged from it with startling clarity, and left him puzzled by the note of reservation he had detected in some of the doctor's comments.

"A very favorable impression, sir," he declared staunchly. "Before the incident at the farm his conduct had always been beyond reproach. Even then, it seems, his only fault was to overestimate this fellow Morvan. That led to disaster, alas, but he can't be blamed entirely—his colleague had proved his worth for several months; anyone would have trusted him completely."

"So that's what you think, is it?" Dr. Fog observed in a noncommittal tone.

"That's my considered opinion, sir."

"So you feel quite confident—as I do, mark you—that he can be entrusted with another mission in enemy-occupied territory?"

"From our point of view, yes. I even think this recent experience of his will stand him in good stead in his future dealings with his subordinates. It remains to be seen whether he'd be willing to go back."

"He has already suggested it," Dr. Fog replied calmly. "He has volunteered a second time."

Disregarding the gasp of admiration Austin had not been able to suppress, he went on to explain:

"On his return, he first went off on leave. Then, as I told you, he was assigned to this unimportant staff job. He languished there for several weeks, forsaken and forgotten, like many casualties in the service, apparently resigned to his fate, filing utterly useless documents during working hours and painting the town red at night, like many other worthy young men who are at present saving the Empire and the civilized world."

"So you know all that as well, sir?" Austin asked quietly.

"I'm interested in the fellow. It's only natural I should follow his career. . . . Well, anyway, he had dropped out of the picture completely when one fine day he wrote at great length to the authorities, asking them to entrust him with another mission in France. Since then he has repeated his application and persisted in his request."

"I bet it was after a night out that he thought of it,

sir! At any rate, after his previous experience, it shows exceptional strength of character."

"No doubt, no doubt," Dr. Fog murmured dryly. "It actually *is* rather unusual. Blusterers who are courageous at a distance—which is already saying something; quite a lot of people aren't courageous even at a distance, let alone at close quarters—usually volunteer once. But once they've had their fingers—or their feet —burned, they're not particularly anxious to have the treatment repeated."

"Volunteering to go back after gambling with death, knowing that the risks are now infinitely greater! And yet you still seem to have some doubt about him, sir?"

"My dear fellow," said the doctor, "far be it from me to curb your enthusiasm, but as far as I'm concerned, you know, volunteers . . ."

He paused, then continued as though he were thinking out loud:

"It's certainly not our business to discourage them. It's splendid, of course, but between ourselves, from the point of view of my special subject, I think I prefer the other sort."

"The other sort?"

"Those who are willing to toe the line. Volunteers . . . I know that some of them are real topnotchers who have a proper idea of their own possibilities; but in most cases, Austin, when they're so overeager to court danger, it's because they're not absolutely sure of their courage and are frightened it might be noticed. They're the worrying kind, frequently found among intellectuals. They're subconsciously trying to delude themselves, and everyone else as well."

"Doesn't that sometimes lead to good results, sir?

Haven't some of those worriers gone beyond the limits of heroism?"

"It has been known," Dr. Fog conceded, "on occasion. Mind you," he went on, changing his tone, "I'm speaking very generally."

He often expressed himself "very generally," as Austin subsequently discovered, particularly with regard to his fellow men.

"But we men of science can't draw up rules for human behavior based on exceptions."

At the doctor's request, and somewhat nettled by his prejudice, Austin got out the file and they began discussing various items in it. One of these was the report Cousin had written when he first arrived in England. Austin, who thought very highly not only of the sentiments it expressed but also of its modest tone and absolute lack of bravado, had been vexed by a marginal note the doctor had made: "Don't forget he *worked* on this report for over a week." He asked his chief to explain exactly what he meant by this and how he came to be so well informed about it.

"It was on my instructions that the security people kept check on every refugee to see how long it took him to write his report, and to note any other relevant details. In Cousin's case I was given quite a lot of useful information. . . . Ten days, Austin, no less than ten days! They had to ask him for it several times; he always wanted to improve on it. And the trouble he took! He started drafting it in the messroom, like everyone else. That wasn't good enough. He couldn't *work* there, you understand. He was disturbed by the others. He wanted to be able to think, to concentrate."

"I see," Austin said pensively.

"Even in his own quarters, he couldn't find the peace and quiet he needed. He was bothered by his two companions. After that he was observed creeping off to some secluded spot on the beach, working away for hours on end, using up an inordinate amount of paper on draft after draft."

"What a shame, sir," Austin observed with a hint of irony in his voice, "that you didn't manage to get hold of one of those drafts. Comparing it with the final fair copy . . ."

"I've got one of them here," the doctor replied calmly. "I forgot to add it to the file. For once I was lucky enough to have an intelligent source of information. You'd be wrong to laugh at these methods. This already shows that our man did not succeed at the first attempt in introducing that note of objectivity and modesty that impressed you so favorably."

Austin read through the draft and lowered his head; but, not being willing to admit defeat, he protested feebly:

"He's a professional writer, sir. It's hardly surprising he should take so much trouble to find the right word."

"The right word—that's just it, Austin. I find no difficulty in picturing him bent over his work, struggling to find the term best suited to put over the idea he wants to express, crossing out, beginning all over again until . . . until perhaps, Austin, the personality of the writer emerges from the text in a manner completely satisfactory to himself."

"In other words, sir, you look upon this document as a work of art."

Dr. Fog heaved a sigh, shrugged his shoulders, and grunted:

"Certainly not. I simply think it's the work of a writer. You don't seem able to understand me at all this morning, my dear fellow!"

They went on discussing the case, and Austin drew attention to Cousin's admirable conduct at the front.

"That isn't literature, anyway, sir. I see you've been able to check up on quite a number of points."

"He always behaved well when he knew he was being watched," Dr. Fog conceded. "I don't deny it."

He gave a brief outline of Cousin's initial activities in the service, then proceeded to the disaster that had put an end to his mission.

Once again it was Cousin's personal report that provided the basic facts; but most of the events described were confirmed by another agent who had been able to get a few details about the raid on the Lachaume farm through a contact in the Gestapo.

Austin had given close attention to this document, which Cousin had submitted after his escape and return to England. It was written in an extremely terse style that at times was almost brutally down-to-earth. It clearly revealed his anxiety not to evade the slightest responsibility, as well as the despair he felt at witnessing the failure of all his endeavors and at seeing his efforts nullified by a moment's weakness on the part of his subordinate.

He gave a brief account of the arrival of the Gestapo, then described in further detail how the Germans had decided to interrogate the prisoners separately. The Gestapo knew what it was doing—in his presence Morvan would not have talked, he was sure of that.

Once they were separated, however, Morvan had not been able to hold out against the brutal treatment. At the last moment, just as the Germans were about to start torturing him, Cousin, Morvan told them everything he knew. And he knew most of the secrets. On that score, Cousin admitted, there was no one to blame but himself. In particular, Morvan knew about the operation scheduled for that night, only fifty kilometers away, against the roundhouse. He had given away this information and a great deal more.

Realizing the urgency of the situation, the Gestapo officer had decided to leave the farm at once with most of his men and organize an ambush for the raiding party, postponing the rest of the interrogation until later. Net result: ten men killed that night, five arrested, and many more casualties in the course of the next few days. To sum up, the whole network was destroyed, six months' work wiped out, and more than fifty patriots tortured and executed.

Cousin went on to describe how he had been taken back to the room where Morvan was lying and was left there with him, guarded by two Gestapo men, to await the officer's return. At this point his style underwent a curious change. The tone became pathetic, betraying a very understandable emotion.

"The next few hours," he wrote, "were the worst I have ever spent in my life. Morvan was stretched out on a bed right in front of me, fully aware of his treachery, I am sure. After throwing a blanket over his legs, the butchers did nothing more for him. In spite of his suffering I could not—no, I could not—feel any pity toward him. It was impossible to forget the harm that was being done as a result of his weakness. In my mind's eye I kept seeing the ghastly massacre that was bound to take place that very night, and it was all his fault.

"As for him, he didn't dare look at me. He kept his eyes shut tight and I could tell his mental agony was more intense than the physical pain. More than once he went through the motions of raising his eyelids, but as soon as he recognized my silhouette he dropped them again. He didn't once open his mouth, and I couldn't bring myself to say a word to him, either."

He resumed his pithy style in describing his escape. During the night his two guards started drinking and eventually passed out. He managed to slip out of his handcuffs, keeping a wary eye on the submachine gun one of the guards had left lying beside him. Cousin's attempt was well timed. In one movement he had sprung to his feet, snatched up the weapon, and mowed down the Gestapo men with a couple of bursts. A chance in a million.

The end of his report dealt briefly with his flight, how he had reached another safe house and eventually managed to get in contact with London. A Lysander had come to take him off one night, after he had received a message ordering him back.

At this juncture Austin interrupted to ask a question, remembering he had noticed something was missing from this description when he had read it over the first time. What had become of Morvan?

"Yes, you're right," the doctor replied slowly. "That part has been omitted, but he gave the details verbally. He was ordered to leave them out of his written report. He had to leave Morvan behind, as he couldn't walk. We also knew from a reliable source that the poor fellow was subsequently killed. The Gestapo officer no doubt took his revenge on him as soon as he got back."

11   "He left him behind!"

Dr. Fog gave a nod.

"Furthermore, he had very good reasons for doing so, which he'll tell you himself. I've asked him to call here this morning."

"Admittedly," Austin muttered, "Morvan was responsible for a ghastly massacre. Just the same . . ."

"Just the same, any court-martial would have acquitted him in view of what he had been through. There would have been no charge brought against him, even by the service itself."

"I suppose he had his cyanide capsule on him and knew what he was meant to do," said Austin, who was already conversant with the customs of the service.

"Perhaps he wasn't able to use it, and besides . . ."

"Yes?"

"I think I can tell you this," said the doctor, after a

moment's hesitation. "We do indeed issue strict instructions on the subject, knowing only too well that they'll hardly ever be followed. Generally speaking, we're not too severe about it."

"There are some, however, who have preferred to die that way."

"There are," Dr. Fog agreed, "but very few."

Austin was about to ask another question, when the house telephone rang. After answering it, the doctor turned back toward him.

"Here's our man."

Austin felt a mounting excitement at the advent of this character who had occupied his thoughts for the past two days. A few minutes later Cousin was shown into the room.

His whole demeanor was perfect, Austin thought. He stood stiffly at attention in front of the doctor, in a deferential attitude but without a trace of servility. He spoke in a crisp, self-confident voice and answered the psychiatrist's questions without equivocation. The doctor had greeted him in an affable manner and spoke to him in an encouraging tone in which Austin once again detected a professional attitude.

He told Cousin that he was fully aware of his splendid record. He could easily understand a man like him being bored to tears in an office. He knew that he had done all he could to get reassigned to active service, and thought perhaps he might be able to employ him.

"That's all I ask, sir," Cousin solemnly replied. "I'm not made for kicking my heels back here in London."

"I am well aware," the doctor went on, "of the outcome of your last mission. It's the sort of thing that could happen to any of us, and I realize you're in no way to blame. I'd like you to tell me the whole story in your own words, however. Nothing like getting to know a man thoroughly when one has to work with him," he added in a wheedling tone that made his young assistant describe him mentally as a monstrous old hypocrite.

Cousin gave his account in a firm voice, without faltering, exactly as he had written it down. By judicious questioning the doctor made him include a few additional details.

It was just at the moment when one of the butchers was bending over him with a red-hot poker in his hand that he heard Morvan cry out in the adjoining room: "Stop, stop! I'll talk! I'll tell you everything, everything! I'll do whatever you wish!" He remembered those dreadful words exactly. He felt like shouting out himself, to tell Morvan to hold his tongue, but the Gestapo man put a gag in his mouth. After that they didn't bother about him any further. They had what they wanted. Morvan went on shouting: "I'll tell you everything, everything! I'll do whatever you want!" Cousin repeated the words grimly.

When he described the hours he subsequently spent in the room with the wretched fellow, his voice, becoming less assured, betrayed the same emotion that had emerged from the corresponding passage in his report. It seemed as though the recollection of that proximity, of his companion's face and visible shame, made him drop his customary reserve in spite of himself. The scene came to life with extraordinary intensity, and Austin had no difficulty in picturing it in all its horror.

Eventually Cousin came to the point at which he had killed the two guards, and paused for a moment. Dr. Fog asked him quietly to go on. He then assumed a calm, almost unfeeling, tone to explain why he had made his escape alone. He looked the doctor straight in the eye, and even, at times, with a sort of defiance.

"He couldn't walk, sir. I would have had to carry him and I wouldn't have gone far. Just then I saw the beam of a headlight in the distance. It was obviously the Gestapo coming back. Dawn was beginning to break. We should both have been caught. You see, sir, I considered I ought not to sacrifice myself pointlessly for the sake of a mere traitor. I left him there. I plunged into the woods alone . . . I'd do it again if I found myself in the same position, sir. I'm willing to answer for my decision before a court-martial, if necessary."

"There's no question of that," Dr. Fog assured him quietly. "This is just a friendly conversation and I fully understand your attitude and your conduct. Let's leave it at that. . . . Incidentally, you know, don't you, that Morvan atoned for his shortcoming? He was killed. The Gestapo shot him."

Cousin hung his head for a moment, then looked up and answered grimly:

"I heard about it. Frankly, sir, I can't bring myself to feel sorry for him. That's too much to expect."

"No one's asking you to," said Dr. Fog.

Cousin's attitude seemed rather tough, to Austin's way of thinking. Yet his state of mind was understandable. After living for months on end under nerve-racking conditions, surrounded by all sorts of danger, successfully eluding the countless traps set by the enemy, and then seeing his efforts suddenly sabotaged, his hopes destroyed by the miserable weakness of a subordinate—all this more than explained his bitterness.

"It's just possible you may be given another mission

in France," Dr. Fog declared after a moment's silence. "I know you won't object to that."

"I couldn't ask for anything better, sir. You *must* give me another chance."

"Austin will keep you posted. Naturally you won't be able to use your own name again. You'll have to change your identity. We've got some experts who'll attend to that. Go and see this one."

He gave him an address, accompanied him as far as the door, and held out his hand.

"Thank you," said Cousin, and that was all.

After he had gone, Dr. Fog subsided into a deep reverie from which Austin made no attempt to rouse him, feeling rather inclined to meditation himself. The doctor seemed to be debating with himself over some serious decision. He came down to earth eventually and made a gesture as though to sweep aside some unwelcome objection.

"The die is cast. We'll send him back, Austin. I'll give you all the details of the role I have in mind for him. I don't want to see him again myself. You're the one who'll give him his orders . . . and keep an eye on him, if necessary," he added lightly.

"I see you still have some reservations about him, sir. That being so, I'm amazed you entrust him with an important mission."

"He may be extremely useful to us in certain circumstances," Dr. Fog replied. "He's intelligent. He's sharp. He has a highly developed psychological sense. You don't find qualities like that every day of the week, and they're just the ones that are needed for the duties I have in mind for him. He won't be given the same field of activity as he had before. He'll be working on his own, in a watertight compartment. Well, not quite alone . . . He'll have someone with him constantly, to witness his actions and make him feel conscious of a watchful eye upon him."

Austin gave a knowing grin, thinking that this role would be entrusted to him. He felt slightly abashed as the doctor went on:

"A reliable colleague who can act as a radio operator."

"I bet you've already found the man you need, sir," said Austin testily.

"A woman, Austin. A couple is always less suspect. Yes, I've already found her. The more I think of it, the more convinced I am that my choice is a good one. With her, I'm pretty sure he'll toe the line. Furthermore, she knows every inch of the region to which I want to send him. It's where she comes from; she's a Breton. But of course, you know her—she's mentioned in our man's file. Can't you guess who it is? Come, come now! I'm referring to Claire."

"Morvan's sister!"

"His sister, exactly. She already belongs to the service. She's an excellent radio operator . . . and she's also volunteered for the field. Don't you think it's a first-rate idea?"

"But sir," exclaimed Austin, who thought it a monstrous choice, "surely you're not going to team her up with Cousin? It's impossible!"

"On the contrary, that's exactly what I plan to do. What's biting you, Austin?"

"Well, sir, I feel . . . I feel it's a sort of confidence trick. If she knew, she'd never accept for a moment."

"Don't worry about that. She does know."

"She knows?"

"She had already heard something about the case, and I've hidden hardly anything from her myself."

"Then she can't possibly be willing to go back with him."

"That's just where you're wrong, my lad," Dr. Fog replied, lowering his voice and assuming a tone full of hidden meaning; "that's just where you're wrong. She has volunteered *twice* to go back with him."

Austin tried to fathom the doctor's inmost thoughts but soon gave it up as a hopeless task. He felt he was being caught in a web of Machiavellian intrigue of which his chief held all the threads and that had been spun with no other consideration than the aim in view. Dr. Fog noticed his uneasiness.

"Don't accuse me of being underhanded. I've talked it over with her at considerable length. As I told you, I've hidden hardly anything from her. The only thing she doesn't know is that Cousin left her brother behind. She believes he was killed in the fray when our man fired on the guards. She would probably volunteer *three* times if I told her the truth, but I didn't go as far as that."

"I'm surprised you didn't, sir," Austin muttered involuntarily.

He blushed at his audacity, but Dr. Fog merely smiled and went on:

"That's not all. We need a brain for this peculiar team, a brain capable of controlling human passion—for there's bound to be some passion between these two; no doubt that's what we need in this type of warfare, but it's not enough for me—someone who can go to

France with them and stay there, at least for a certain length of time: a sound brain. I thought of you."

"I'm at your service, sir."

Austin's indignation could not last in the face of the exhilarating prospect of taking part in this venture. He was about to express himself in warmer terms when the doctor gruffly interrupted him.

"Above all, don't tell me you're also volunteering. I've selected you for the job, that's all."

"At your service, sir."

"That's settled, then. . . . Just the same, I should like to be sure that you're accepting this willingly."

"With the best will in the world, sir," the young man exclaimed with an eagerness that brought a smile to the lips of his chief.

"That's fine. This evening we'll work out the details of the mission and I'll introduce you to Claire. I'm sure you'll like her. Knows her own mind. Quite a character, I should imagine."

"I don't doubt it, sir. I can guess what's behind her attitude. She can't bear the idea of her brother's having failed, and she wants to make up for him, redeem the family name. It's admirable."

Dr. Fog gave him a deep, penetrating look and said in a strange voice:

"You're extremely perspicacious, young man. Incidentally, I forgot to tell you, but you've probably realized it already—she simply adored her brother. She adored him, Austin, and was full of admiration for him."

From the way the doctor underlined these last words, he seemed to expect some reply. But none came. Austin remained silent, disconcerted by a vague suspicion of some ulterior motive on the doctor's part that was too subtle for him to understand. Dr. Fog did not press the point and dismissed him. Just as Austin was leaving, the doctor tapped his forehead.

"I almost forgot . . . Have you found a suitable name for our man?"

"Not yet, sir. I haven't given it much thought."

"Well, you know, last night I had a rather bright idea," he said with an air of false modesty. "I thought of Arvers. How does that strike you?"

"Arvers?"

"*Mon âme a son secret,** " the doctor declaimed in the same self-satisfied tone. "I'm not quite sure what put the idea into my head. . . . Yet I can't imagine a better name for him—Arvers."

He looked as though he had made a most valuable discovery, and Austin could not help thinking, as he left the room, that the devil himself sometimes has a childish side to his nature.

* Translator's note: *"Mon âme a son secret, ma vie a son mystère"* is the first line of the so-called "Sonnet d'Arvers"—the only sonnet written by the nineteenth-century poet of that name.

12   The mission for which Arvers had been selected was extremely simple. So it seemed, at least, to Austin, who kept wondering over and over again if it wasn't perhaps a pretext for one of Dr. Fog's secret designs. He could scarcely see the reason for sending two agents into France (plus himself, whose only function was to supervise the others) and organizing a parachute drop by night—always a tricky operation—merely for Arvers to establish contact with a German who was prepared to sell some information to the Allies.

The instructions Arvers had been given could be summed up as follows: as soon as he landed in France he was to settle in a certain villa in the vicinity of the Rance—by a strange coincidence, not far from Morvan's village, where his mother undoubtedly was still living. This was to be his regular meeting place with Gleicher, the German traitor, an industrialist who had a neighboring villa he visited from time to time. Cousin would receive whatever information there was and pay for it according to its importance. The villa had already been rented and Gleicher had been notified to get in touch with him, which said a great deal for the means at Dr. Fog's disposal and made his reason for sending an additional agent there all the more incomprehensible. Any urgent information could be signaled back by radio. A messenger would come at regular intervals to collect the bulkier documents. Arvers, in fact, would simply be acting as a letter box.

Meanwhile Austin was to remain in the background, without entering into communication with the German. His mission was to supervise the team and see that it functioned properly. Dr. Fog's main interest was in Arvers: his conduct and his reactions under certain circumstances. He discussed this at some length with Austin, without giving him any definite instructions but drawing his attention to the points he considered most significant.

"The essential problem in this world, and particularly for us, Austin, is the interaction of the mental and the physical, of the body and the mind. What I want to know is how he deals with this problem."

Austin set to work with youthful ardor and a natural curiosity that the doctor's methods had sharpened considerably. He scarcely let Arvers out of his sight during the time devoted to their preparations. On the eve of their departure he wanted to let the doctor know certain things that had come to his notice, but the doctor cut him short. He simply asked him if he thought everything would be all right and, on receiving an affirmative reply, wished him good luck and dismissed him. There were other matters claiming his attention.

And so Austin was parachuted into France with the incongruous couple. He spent three months there, exchanging no more than a few brief signals with his chief in London. By the end of that time Arvers and Claire had settled at the villa, passing themselves off as young newlyweds. Claire, who was well known in the neighborhood, had kept her true identity. It was believed that she had eloped into the Free Zone with her lover and had returned to the fold after marrying him. Their personal papers were up to date and in order.

Gleicher, the German source of information, came down at regular intervals to spend a weekend in the villa next door, the only other house within a radius of about a mile, and his meetings with Arvers occurred under ideal conditions of security. Claire sent the information back by radio, operating either from the villa or from the back parlor of Mrs. Morvan's grocery. Her mother, whom she had contacted at once, was the only person in the area who knew of her clandestine activities. The old woman had offered her help, and, after a certain amount of hesitation, Arvers had agreed to accept her assistance. It was to her house that the messenger came from time to time to collect the reports, since Arvers had no direct dealings with this agent. Dr. Fog had insisted on this point. The experts in London appeared to be quite satisfied with the information that had been collected thus far.

Austin, who was living in Rennes in a safe house that was also unknown to Arvers, met the couple from time to time at a secret rendezvous and saw for himself that they were both doing their jobs. He felt there was nothing more for him to do and was relieved when he received a signal from Dr. Fog asking him to come back to London if he thought the situation no longer required his presence in France. Since this was, in fact, his considered opinion, he made the necessary arrangements for his return, and a light airplane flew in one night to take him back.

The following morning found him once again in Dr. Fog's office. Contrary to the attitude of indifference he had shown on the eve of Austin's departure, the doctor actually now seemed impatient to hear what he had to say and to know the results of his supervision. He asked Austin not to omit a single significant detail.

"I'd better begin, sir, with the period we spent at the parachute training center prior to the drop. It was only a few days, just long enough for some preliminary training and five practice jumps, but we were hardly out of one another's sight for a moment."

"Good," said the doctor; "go on. A man's reactions at the prospect of a parachute jump are most important. It's usually an extremely instructive experience and makes a deep impression on certain temperaments. I've known perfectly brave men who were incapable of launching themselves out of an aircraft. I remember putting a certain captain through this test—a real tough fellow, I assure you. He had proved his courage countless times. Well . . ."

He spoke of these tests and trials as though they were simple laboratory experiments. Austin could not help smiling now at this old familiar manner of his, which once had made him feel so uneasy.

"Well," the doctor continued, "it was utterly pitiful,

a dreadful exhibition. The whole team was ashamed of him. When he was given the order to jump, he clung to the nearest man, the nearest object, anything he could get hold of. He was clawing at the fuselage with his nails. When he saw they were going to heave him out by force, he implored them—yes, he actually implored them with tears in his eyes—to let him off. He was reduced to an absolute jelly, Austin, and yet, as I said before, the fellow was a hero."

"Nothing like that happened to Arvers, sir—or to me, for that matter, though I certainly didn't enjoy it, I assure you. As for the girl, sir, I may as well tell you right away, I have nothing but admiration."

"Really?"

Austin seemed to recall his own experience as a parachutist with anything but pleasure.

"To be permanently as calm and cool as she was during that sort of ordeal, you've either got to be an insensitive brute, which she obviously isn't, or else be uplifted, anesthetized, by some sentiment sufficiently deep and powerful to make a mockery of fear and deaden your reactions to it."

"Didn't I tell you there was bound to be some passion in our team?" said Dr. Fog.

"She was perfectly *detached*, sir—that's the only word for it: detached. During those few days I'm sure she didn't once give a thought to the fact that she would have to launch herself into the void at a height of three thousand feet. Her courage came to her quite naturally; it didn't entail the slightest effort. Her appetite wasn't affected, she spoke in her usual tone of voice and didn't have much to say. She looked on this stage of the training as an insignificant formality. . . . A one-track

mind, in which there was no room for any sensation—
that's the impression she gave me, sir."

"Perhaps it's just an exalted feeling of patriotism?"

"Perhaps," Austin replied, in the same tone of disbelief the doctor had used to make this suggestion.

They looked at each other in silence for a moment,
then Austin observed pointedly:

"She never took her eyes off him."

"Really?"

"Not for a minute, sir; not for a second."

"That doesn't surprise me unduly," Dr. Fog said
thoughtfully. "But what about him? Let's hear about
him for a change."

"He behaved like a brave man, if that's what you
want to know. I could give you some details . . ."

"That's the stuff!" the doctor cried eagerly. "Let's
get on to the details."

"The day before our first jump, during the afternoon, in the course of exit practice from an aircraft on
the ground, I began to detect certain symptoms in him:
fits of absent-mindedness, sudden attacks of pallor—all
very normal under the circumstances. That evening,
during dinner, I'm sure he had no appetite at all, and
yet . . ."

"Yes?"

Austin went on, his brows furrowed in a visible effort to recall the scene.

"He took a big helping . . . and it wasn't what he
had intended to do, I noticed that. He was going to
pass the dish on, after taking no more than a spoonful,
when his eyes met Claire's. I told you she never let any
of his gestures escape her, not even at mealtimes. He
changed color at once and his features seemed to

shrivel. He took the dish back and gave himself an enormous helping."

"Excellent," Dr. Fog said, rubbing his hands together. "And did he eat it all?"

"At first I thought he wouldn't be able to manage it; he could hardly lift his fork to his mouth and he had difficulty in chewing. I could see what an effort he was having to make, and it wasn't hard to visualize the painful progress of the food down his throat. Each mouthful made him shudder from head to foot. At one moment his arm dropped to his side, as though it had lost all feeling. He seemed to be at his last gasp."

"Excellent," the doctor again remarked. "I see you kept him under close observation."

"Not nearly as close as she did, sir, not nearly as close!" Austin exclaimed in a sudden fever of excitement. "Heavens, she seemed to be gobbling him up with her eyes! When he sat back in his chair like that, inert and on the point of fainting, she leaned over toward him like some beast of prey. It was dreadful, sir, I assure you. I was just going to make some remark to put an end to the business, when he noticed her. He sat up at once with a start. All his muscles contracted, and he managed to resume a more or less normal manner. Then he gave a gulp, and not only swallowed the mouthful that had stuck in his throat but finished up everything on his plate as well. But after that he turned very pale. He smiled—yes, he managed to smile—and mumbled a word of apology. Then he got up and left the room.

"She followed him with her eyes, her body still leaning in his direction as though attracted by a magnet. He came back a few minutes later. I'm sure he had gone out to be sick. He was as pale as ever, but he was still smiling. He sat down again. His eyes met Claire's. He assumed an air of defiance . . . the same sort of manner he put on the following day, after the first jump, when he asked to be allowed to do another right away."

The doctor, who seemed intensely interested in this account of the meal, interrupted him.

"Just a moment. This is absolutely fascinating. Don't go on so fast. We were still at dinner . . ."

"At dinner, that's right," said Austin, who seemed to be curiously moved by the recollection of that scene. "Well, he looked her straight in the eyes and . . . Do you know what he did then, sir? You'd never believe it."

"I think I can guess," Dr. Fog replied calmly.

"He took a second helping! Do you realize that, sir? He took a second helping, and not a small one, either!"

13 "So he took a second helping, did he?" Dr. Fog repeated.

There were at least two unusual elements in this dialogue: the vehement manner in which Austin was reporting these trivial details, and the deep attention with which the doctor was listening, each man seeming to attribute a tremendous significance to the petty incidents.

"I can see him now, sir. He had pulled himself together. With a courteous gesture he offered the dish first to Claire and then to me, and when we refused he helped himself again.

"That's all, as far as the meal goes, sir. But I took advantage of that evening, when we were all together, to brief him on his mission. He was very disappointed and could not help saying so. He had applied for an active post, he told me. That was what he wanted—

action. He repeated the word several times, with fierce insistence. I explained that we attached great importance to the contact with Gleicher and hinted that there might be some action as a result of it. He acquiesced. Then I got down to the details: how to justify their presence in the villa. I outlined my plan to both of them: they were to be a young married couple who wanted to find a little peace and quiet in the remote countryside."

"I let you have a free hand on that score. So you decided they would be able to act their parts convincingly?"

"I was still of two minds about it, but that evening I was struck by the way she kept watching him all the time, with a jealous, anxious eye, and by his reactions to this."

"I see," said the doctor, rubbing his hands together. "So you told them . . ."

"I assumed my most cloak-and-dagger manner, sir, and said: 'From the moment you arrive in France, in fact, from this moment on, you have to behave at all times like a couple hopelessly in love. The war doesn't mean a thing to you. Your one and only thought is for each other. This must be apparent in every gesture you make, in every word you utter.' "

Dr. Fog gave his young colleague a look of surprise, tinged with admiration.

"You told them that?"

"Wasn't I right? Didn't they have to live the part completely?"

"Absolutely. And they followed your instructions?"

"To the letter, sir, with amazing success."

"You didn't suggest they should share the same bed, did you?"

"I didn't go quite as far as that, sir," said Austin.

The two men looked at each other in silence, then Austin went on, with the curious animation that seized him whenever he spoke about Claire.

"But I'm positive she would have raised no objection, sir. She is obsessed by one idea and nothing else, I'm certain. She would go to bed with the Loch Ness monster if it served the purpose she has in mind—she would even go to bed with him, perhaps, and with the same detachment she displayed during her parachute training."

"What about him?"

"I didn't bring up the question. All that matters is their outward behavior, and they're both so conscientious about this that no one could ever suspect their true feelings. Their attitudes would deceive anyone who saw them. The sort of passionate interest she shows in him and which she betrays by endless furtive or piercing glances; the uneasy manner in which he, for his part, responds to this constant surveillance—all this had suddenly struck me, as I said before. It could easily be interpreted as a sign of being deeply in love. I think I've made the best use of their natural reactions, sir, as you advised me to do."

"I'm beginning to wonder if you're not even craftier than I am, young man," Dr. Fog said pensively. "I foresee a brilliant career for you."

"A strange couple, sir," said Austin, who was still deeply moved by certain recollections. "I can imagine them now, alone together in the intimacy of that villa tucked away in the woods, both of them submerged in their own thoughts. . . ."

"Not so fast, not so fast!" Dr. Fog protested. "What about the training jumps?"

"Those all went off perfectly well. . . . I'll go straight on now to the actual drop into France, sir, if you don't mind. It was no different from the training jumps. It's a curious fact—and the professionals all confirm this—but you never get used to the horror of it."

"The horror? Really?" Dr. Fog remarked in a completely detached tone of voice.

"Unadulterated horror, sir. The fifth is just as bad as the first, and the hundredth as bad as the fiftieth, so they say. Whether you jump at three thousand feet or at ten thousand, over a flat plain or over a range of mountains, whether you're greeted on landing with a cup of tea or with a burst from a machine gun, the agony's always the same. But to come back to him . . . He was as white as a sheet, in England as well as over enemy territory, but he jumped all right."

"What about her?"

"Absolutely indifferent. I wouldn't have believed it was possible. . . . But there's something else I must tell you about him.

"Before we took off, while we were waiting in the mess, I noticed he was turning paler and paler. All the color was gradually draining from his cheeks. Over the Channel, after the dispatcher had given us permission to smoke, I caught a glimpse of his face by the light of a match. I almost let out a scream. I don't think any shroud has ever concealed a more ghastly sight. Yet in the dark there was nothing to betray the state he was in—or almost nothing. He even managed to utter a word or two now and then, and unless you were watching as closely as I was, you would never have noticed the effort it cost him—a superhuman effort, no doubt. Another thing I remember—and, at the time, I considered it heroic—in order to prove he was in complete command of himself and was capable of following my instructions under all circumstances, up there, in the aircraft, he made a point of keeping up his cover story. He treated Claire with great affection, showered her with attentions, and murmured words of encouragement that were quite unnecessary as far as she was concerned. Such an absolute discrepancy between his outward behavior and the death mask I had glimpsed . . . I could hardly believe my eyes, sir!"

"But he jumped all right?"

"He jumped all right, but during the few seconds before the green light went on I thought he was going to collapse. I had had a bet with myself . . . because I, too, needed to think about something else. I couldn't actually see his features, but their tautness created a sort of tension in the immediate atmosphere. Honestly, sir, the thundering of his heart seemed to be making the whole fuselage vibrate. I said something to him; he was incapable of answering me. That was all, sir. The dispatcher didn't notice a thing. No one did, apart from me—and Claire as well, of course; because, like me, only more intently, she was observing those minute signs of fear in the dark. She was sitting there, leaning toward him. She was waiting, she was hoping, hoping wildly . . . Oh, sir, now I know, now I realize what she's hoping for—but of course you know it perfectly well yourself!"

Dr. Fog nodded without answering and asked him to go on.

"When the green light came on and he heard the word 'Go!', for a fraction of a second, but no more than that, he hesitated. I felt his fate was sealed; at that instant I thought I had won my bet. And she, too, believed she had been right. That was all she was thinking of, sir! The horror of the drop meant nothing to her. I could almost hear the cry of triumph she was about to give but which never passed her lips—he had jumped. I'm convinced he sensed the violence of her feelings just as I did. She was leaning right over toward him and, in that confined space, a sort of magnetic field had developed that established a sort of telepathy between us. That's what launched him out of the aircraft, sir . . . Then we jumped out after him."

14   Austin wanted to give a few details about their arrival: how they had successfully joined up together after landing in the dark, how they had reached the house safely, how the couple had moved into the villa, and how Gleicher had contacted them. He soon saw, however, that this was of no interest to Dr. Fog, who brought the conversation back to his favorite subject—Arvers and his reactions in certain tricky situations.

"I haven't much to tell you, sir. But I happened by chance to witness a rather telling scene. I mean the incident with the drunken German soldier; it might have turned out badly. It has nothing to do with our mission and is of no interest except from the psychological point of view."

"You know that anything to do with the psychological aspect is meat and drink to me," Dr. Fog said gruffly. "Come on, let's hear about your drunken German soldier."

Austin embarked on his story without further ado.

"It was shortly after they moved in. I had to get in touch with them one day and had arranged to meet them at Rennes, outside the big movie house there. What we usually did was to buy our tickets together so as to have adjoining seats. I turned up well ahead of time and decided to wait in the café next door. I had just sat down in the far corner when they came into the place together. They had also arrived early and had had the same idea. I didn't announce my presence. I was hidden from them by a partition, but by leaning forward a little, I could see them without being seen myself."

Dr. Fog voiced his approval of this maneuver.

"Splendid. It's not often you get a chance to observe people without their knowing it."

"I was able to see immediately that they were both following my instructions scrupulously, even in this place where they were unknown. To all outward appearances, they were a typical couple of young lovers. For a moment, sir, I was almost taken in by it myself. A strange thought suddenly came into my head. I began to wonder if they weren't actually in earnest."

"Odder situations than that have been known to develop," said Dr. Fog, "but as far as this particular pair is concerned, it would surprise me."

"It would surprise me too, sir. Anyway, this suspicion was soon dispelled.

"Time went by. I was about to settle my bill and move on to our rendezvous ahead of them, when the German soldier came in. He was blind drunk and his arrival caused an uneasy stir in the café. He settled down at the counter facing them and ordered a drink, which the waiter reluctantly served him. Then he turned around toward the couple and began staring at them intently. His attitude was so insolent that the waiter stopped clearing up the glasses to look at him.

"I postponed my departure and waited, anxious to see how Arvers would behave. He had become quite red in the face and was pretending, against all probability, not to notice the drunk's attitude. He had turned his head in another direction and appeared to be deeply absorbed in the contemplation of a large clock.

"When the soldier taunted him out loud, he again changed color and became almost as white as he had been in the airplane. Jerking his chin in Claire's direction, the German then made an obscene remark in broken French. Arvers' features contracted, though he still could not bring himself to turn around and face the fellow."

"A profoundly interesting test," Dr. Fog observed. "I've always wondered how he would react in a hand-to-hand fight. His file doesn't give the slightest indication on that point."

"There's something still more curious to come, sir. It was when I looked at Claire that I had a real surprise.

"Her behavior was extraordinary. Instead of remaining aloof, as she usually was and as any woman might have, she gave a quick sidelong smile that was a direct invitation to the brute's advances. There was no mistaking it. Each glance of hers was an encouragement for him to persist in his taunts. She even made a gesture of contempt in her companion's direction, shrugging her shoulders and looking the drunkard straight in the eyes. The waiter, who couldn't help noticing her behavior, showed his indignation by clattering the glasses together.

"Arvers, whose head was turned in the opposite direction, could not maintain that position indefinitely. He turned around toward her just as the soldier, incited by her gestures, was making a direct obscene proposal to her. Arvers happened to be saying something to her at that very instant. He broke off in the middle of the sentence and I could guess what the gist of it was. He was alluding to our meeting and was telling her, with feigned indifference, that it was time for them to be moving if they didn't want to be late. I haven't forgotten a single detail of the scene, sir. He stopped short, his voice died away as his gaze fell on the girl, whose smile, originally aimed at the German, changed its target as well as its meaning. It was at him her smile was now directed, taunting, full of scorn. Then his face became even whiter and I distinctly saw his leg begin to tremble.

"She looked at him like this for several seconds, then she herself said something. Her voice betrayed utter contempt as well as intense satisfaction. . . . I don't know if I'm making myself clear, sir."

"Nothing could be clearer," said the doctor. "I can see the whole thing as though I were there myself."

"It was the outcome that surprised me," Austin went on. "There again I lost a bet with myself. . . . Anyway, she said something in reply to his remark.

" 'You're right, darling,' she said . . . Did I tell you

she always called him 'darling'? Oh, I can just see them there by themselves in the villa. Ours is a dirty job, sir, there's no getting away from it!"

"You realize that," said the doctor, "just when you're beginning to have a passion for this job. So she said to him: 'You're right, darling . . .' "

"She said it with withering contempt, underscoring each word. 'You're right, darling, we must be leaving. It's high time we got out of here.' And she rose to her feet.

" 'Just a moment,' Arvers exclaimed suddenly.

"I gave a start. His voice, which had altered abruptly, seemed to belong to someone else and I stupidly peered around the room. No, it was certainly he, but his attitude had undergone a complete change. Only a moment before, he had been little more than a dummy; now he had an air of authority. I also observed—I think I'm beginning to be quite a good observer, sir—I also observed that the nervous tremor in his leg had stopped. His gestures were deliberate, but somehow stiff and mechanical. . . . An automaton, that's it—an automaton obeying an impulse, an external will. The shock of the girl's scorn had caused this metamorphosis.

" 'Just a moment, darling,' he said, motioning her to sit down again.

"He stepped around the table, walked straight across to the soldier, who was watching him with a smirk, stopped in front of him, and gave him a hard slap in the face. Then he went back to her, and there was a glint of triumph in his eyes. Meanwhile she lowered her head and looked extremely disappointed. After that . . . after that, sir, he seemed to collapse, inert and defenseless in the face of his adversary, incapable, I felt, of retaliating in any way had he been attacked. The trembling in his leg had started up again. I held my breath."

"A dramatic moment, I should imagine," said Dr. Fog.

"The tension was dispelled, luckily, by the attitude of the very man responsible for it. The soldier looked disconcerted and shaken for a moment, then burst into a loud guffaw. He was too drunk to fight back. He murmured 'friend,' then turned his back and went on with his drink.

"'We can leave now, darling,' Arvers said with a tremor in his voice over which he had no control. He was at the end of his rope. She got up to join him. I watched them move off arm in arm, while the waiter gave him an obsequious bow."

"So on the whole you're pleased with your team?" Dr. Fog asked.

"Fairly pleased, sir, although Claire's attitude worries me somewhat. But I'm not so satisfied with my own role."

"Each man to his own job. What's bothering you?"

For the last moment or two Austin had been looking slightly vexed. He decided to ask the question that was preying on his mind.

"It's this, sir. Has she been given a private briefing from you without my knowing it?"

"What do you mean?"

"Have you given her instructions to keep an eye on him, to spy on him?"

"No, Austin," the doctor replied frankly, "I'm relying on you for that. But I knew she would do so in any case, and I think it may be useful. I suppose you no longer have the slightest doubt about the motive for her conduct?"

"Not the slightest!" Austin exclaimed. "I was mad to think her intention was to redeem her brother's crime. What an idea! Not once has she acknowledged his treachery. Not for a second has she believed him guilty."

"Not for a second. I've known that all along, but I felt it was better for you to find it out for yourself."

"She has only one idea, sir, one ambition—to prove her brother's innocence. But in that case, if he really was innocent, if he wasn't the one who talked . . ."

He stopped short. After a short pause Dr. Fog put his thought into words.

"Someone talked, Austin. If it wasn't Morvan . . ."

"It's impossible, sir. Why should Cousin have been so anxious to go back? He was sitting pretty over here and could have ended the war at his desk."

The doctor nodded pensively but did not reply to this question.

"Well, anyway," he said, "you mustn't be surprised if she seizes every opportunity to test his courage and plumb its depths."

"She doesn't merely seize opportunities, she goes out of her way to create them. That's exactly what's worrying me. She doesn't give a damn for the war or for the enemy."

"Neither does he, perhaps," said Dr. Fog, "and that's where we come in. It's up to us to channel these passions in such a manner as to serve the interests of the country. And with that end in view, I think it's essential he should feel he is being watched."

"Watched, sir! What you mean is spied on, tracked down, hunted! First of all by me—he must have guessed what I was up to over there. If you could only have seen what he was like, knowing he was being observed at every instant, hesitating to make the most commonplace gesture for fear of its being interpreted as a sign of weakness, forcing himself to divest his conduct of anything that could give the slightest suggestion of fear. Can you imagine anything more ghastly, sir, than having to assume the reactions of a hero every moment of the day?"

"That's what we need in this service, Austin," Dr. Fog replied quietly. "Men who behave as though they were heroes, whatever the circumstances."

"There they are, living together, and he has to treat her the whole time like a wife he adores. . . . And that's not his only worry."

"Of course not. There are also the agent's natural enemies—the Gestapo and the *Abwehr*. But he volunteered for the job."

"I wasn't thinking of them—what I mean is, her mother. She knows all about it."

"I'm sure she does. What is she like?"

"She doesn't have much to say, but I'd swear she's even worse than her daughter, sir. She'd do her damnedest to vindicate her son. A forceful personality, what's more. I have a feeling that Claire's a mere child compared to her mother."

"You were quite right to accept her services."

"Perhaps. But I wouldn't be in Arvers' shoes for anything in the world."

"Nor would I," Dr. Fog agreed. "But then . . ."

He assumed a strange tone of voice and looked directly at Austin as he added:

"But then, I shouldn't have liked to be in Morvan's, either."

PART THREE

PART THREE

15   Arvers opened his eyes with a start as he heard the shutters bang in the adjoining room. Even before recovering consciousness, he felt the painful spasm in all his organs, and the discomfort of his body aggravated that of his uneasy mind. It was the sort of horrible awakening he experienced every morning: for several minutes at this time of day the physical and the mental would react on each other with the pitiless regularity of a machine.

A faint light filtered into the room. Among the objects just beginning to come into focus, the heating stove directly opposite his bed appeared to him once again as an evil phantom placed there by the hand of a demon to remind him of some distant hell. He would gladly have got rid of the wretched contraption, he would at least have moved it to some other position so as not to have it before his eyes on waking up, but he did not dare: Claire would have been sure to notice. Her twisted, hostile imagination would have seized on this simple gesture and read some sinister meaning into it. He was fully aware of the malevolence of her constant spying.

He listened to her footsteps in the adjoining room and trembled as they approached the connecting door. It was the sound of her shutters being flung open that had waked him. She made no attempt to open them quietly —rather the opposite, in fact. She knew he never managed to get to sleep until it was almost dawn, and did her utmost to allow him no rest. When the sound of her footsteps ceased, he imagined her standing motionless and intent, her eyes fixed on his room, listening to the sound of his breathing.

He got out of bed cautiously, taking care not to make the springs creak, and tiptoed over to the hiding place where he kept a bottle of cheap Calvados. He took several minutes to turn the key in the drawer, casting anxious glances in the direction of the door. He silently took a couple of mouthfuls, careful not to let the liquid gurgle in the bottle. If she had suspected he regularly took a nip of alcohol first thing in the morning, she would have been certain to infer that he was lacking in innate courage.

After finishing his drink, he stood motionless for a moment, waiting for the comforting fumes to rise to his head. Then he put the bottle back with the same care, but with a steadier hand, and went back to bed again. The alcohol was not sufficient in itself to dispel the unbearable sensation that her distrust caused him, but it acted as a catalyst on his mind—that mind which alone had the power to concoct the antidotes against the poison that was consuming him.

He managed to summon enough strength to revive his favorite fantasies and re-create the image of his ideal hero. Every morning he forced himself to make this mental effort, which for him took the place of prayer and from which he derived fresh strength to continue the daily struggle.

He fell to dreaming. He had no need to improve on reality to make the torrent of glory he needed spring forth from his adventures. He merely had to focus a spotlight on certain aspects for them to become immediately so brilliant as to outshine the few insignificant details that were consequently lost in the shadows. He had practised these mental gymnastics for so long now that he performed them automatically. . . . Was he not a secret-service agent of outstanding ability and daring? Had he not succeeded, thanks to his own resourcefulness, in escaping his redoubtable foe, the Gestapo? Having gotten back to London—a unique feat, he knew, in the annals of the service—had he not insisted on returning to the hell he had only just left, even though the danger was magnified tenfold by his previous arrest? His superiors had been amazed, and yet they were only too familiar with acts of courage. They had wanted to restrain him, to save him from his own temerity. He had had only to say the word—not even that, he had had only to stay put and say nothing—to have seen the war out in a staff appointment. He had rejected this security and plunged voluntarily once more into the abyss. He had dropped by night from a plane into a country where the worst possible dangers awaited him. All this was true; no one could deny it.

And yet his superiors did not show him the consideration he deserved and expected. Faced with these proofs of his courage, they should have entrusted him with a task involving the highest responsibilities. He felt he was capable of being Number One in the service for the whole of France.

He brooded for some time over his present functions, trying to persuade himself that his contact with Gleicher was of extreme importance to the conduct of the war and that this mission was a mark of the esteem in which he was held by his superiors. He succeeded in this endeavor fairly often, but this morning the effort was too great for his physical resources. He could not blind himself to certain obvious signs of reserve in this respect: an incomprehensible, unjustified reserve that was intolerable to a man of his character and that, so obsessively conscious of it was he, impeded the fruition of his dreams of glory.

Dr. Fog had congratulated him, to be sure, but he had assigned him to a subordinate position. This fellow Austin, a mere stripling, was in command. Austin was the one in charge of the general organization, over and above him. True, he was allowed a certain initiative in his dealings with Gleicher, but all the other arrangements were made without consulting him. He knew nothing about the messenger who came to fetch the mail. Claire herself took it around to her mother's place. Of course, this method seemed reasonable from the security point of view: it was only natural for Claire to go and call on her mother quite often. Just the same, Austin might have consulted him before coming to this decision. Why hadn't he done so? Was it possible that they did not consider him absolutely *reliable?*

Try as he might, he could not get rid of this horrible idea, and the thought of Morvan's mother added to his dismay. He had met her only once, but he could not bear the way she had looked at him. He never went into the village. It was quite enough, having to live with the daughter.

His dreams were taking a decidedly gloomy turn. He toyed with the idea of having another swig of alcohol but changed his mind for fear his breath might betray him. He got out of bed, this time making no pretense about it, and opened the shutters. The view of the neighboring town he could see through the trees suggested a more engaging theme for his thoughts, and he managed to derive a little comfort from the prospect of his next meeting with Gleicher. The German was to come down the following day and would hurry around, as usual, to get in touch with him. Arvers took infinite pleasure in making him feel his superiority and, in his company, experienced moments of almost complete euphoria. He despised Gleicher wholeheartedly—a man of the lowest type, who betrayed his country for money. Arvers never missed an opportunity to show the German what he thought of him, and his pleasure was twice as great when the meeting took place in front of Claire.

16   As he left the restaurant in the Champs
Élysées where he had treated himself to a delicious
meal including five French wines, for which he had a
weakness, Gleicher saw that he still had several hours
before catching the train for Rennes. A car would be
waiting for him there, and it would be dark by the time
he reached the villa where he spent an occasional week
end. He had finished all his other business in Paris. All
that remained was to prepare for his meeting with
Arvers, which he always did with particular care.

He walked along at a leisurely pace until he came to
a modest building in the Quartier de l'Europe. It was
here he had set up his office; although he was in a position to requisition the most sumptuous house, he preferred to be discreet. The building had no elevator.
With his brief case under his arm, he walked up the
three flights of stairs at a fairly brisk pace but without

being able to conceal his slight limp. He was a heavily built man in his fifties, bald and wearing spectacles—to all outward appearances, one of those German businessmen engaged in industry or finance who frequently visited Paris, were absorbed in their work, but were not averse to the pleasures that were available in the capital at bargain prices. His official position was inscribed on the door, which he reached slightly out of breath—"Reinforced Concrete Construction. Inspector's Office"—a civilian job that accounted for his knowledge of important military secrets.

As he climbed the last few steps, his appearance underwent a slight change. His back stiffened, his stomach seemed to decrease in volume; his limp assumed a different aspect. He went in without knocking, left his hat in the hall, and entered one of the two rooms constituting the office. Otto rose to his feet as he came in. Otto, his assistant, must have been about the same age as himself. The formality of his greeting was in the true German tradition and appeared faintly incongruous against the background of a business concern.

Gleicher's features now showed an authority that was not apparent in the street and still less so in the restaurant. Before sitting down in the chair Otto had just vacated, he placed his spectacles on a corner of the desk. He did not need them here.

"Is the *Spielmaterial* ready?" he asked.

"Yes, Herr Doktor. Our special branch let me have it this morning."

The "Herr Doktor" was odious to the ears of Colonel Count von Gleicher, ex-officer of the Wehrmacht, who had been persuaded to transfer to the *Abwehr* as a result of a nasty wound and the friendship of Admiral

Canaris. If this form of address was necessary in front of others, Otto, he felt, might at least address him by his military rank when they were alone together. He had often felt like mentioning this but had demurred for fear of being thought ridiculous. Otto, however, seemed to stress the "Herr Doktor" intentionally, as though his purpose was to make an amateur aware of the rigors of the job at which he himself was a seasoned professional.

"Is it all right?" he asked, taking a pile of documents his assistant handed to him.

Otto pursed his lips and remarked pompously:

"It's not too bad, I suppose. As usual, all the information is plausible and quite a lot of it—what we know to be already in the hands of the enemy—is accurate. Just the same, Herr Doktor, if this business develops as we hope, our technicians will have to make a greater effort."

"Really?"

"The British services responsible for interpreting the *Spielmaterial* are also fairly astute, Herr Doktor," Otto said with an air of great experience. "In my opinion it would be advisable to ask the head of our special branch to see that the next supply shows some improvement."

"Right," the Herr Doktor replied gruffly. "I'll do so in good time, if it proves to be necessary. Meanwhile I'll just glance through this."

As he bent over the file, Otto went on:

"I feel it's even more important, Herr Doktor, since the Arvers affair might eventually be extremely interesting. There's some new information about his character."

In spite of himself, Gleicher pricked up his ears.

"It's a long story, which our service seems to have pieced together pretty well, Herr Doktor. It's like this . . ."

"If it's a long story, you'd better tell it to me later. Let me get on with these documents first."

Otto was beginning to get on his nerves. In the respectful manner in which he made certain suggestions, in the way he uttered the words "our special branch," Gleicher detected only too clearly a feeling of condescension toward a regimental officer who had become his chief by force of circumstance but who would never be as familiar as he was with the finer points of clandestine organization. Ex-Colonel von Gleicher was not displeased to be offered this opportunity to put him in his place. Having done so, however, he realized he himself was being somewhat touchy, and he tempered his severity with a joke.

"After all, I'd better know something about the intelligence I'm going to hand over to the enemy!"

Otto acquiesced and waited for his chief to finish reading through the file. Gleicher devoted a great deal of attention and care to this task, turning each detail over in his mind, jotting down notes and occasionally asking his assistant for further explanations. Since there was one point that was still unclear, Otto, at his request, had a long conversation with one of the technicians in the section that manufactured information designed, in secret-service jargon, to "deceive" the enemy. Gleicher was a sensitive man and was eager to prove that he did not fulfill his functions like an amateur, as Otto sometimes seemed to think. Entering into the character of the Herr Doktor, he had forced himself to study the technicalities of reinforced concrete construction, with special reference to fortifications, which he was supposed to inspect. He wanted to be sure that no question on this subject would find him without an answer.

When everything was clear to him, he placed the papers methodically in his brief case.

"I'll run through them again in the train," he muttered. "Now then, Otto, let's hear your story about our friend Herr Arvers."

17   "I'll have to go back quite a bit, Herr Doktor. You remember that business about the Cousin network and the Lachaume farm?"

"As though I could ever forget it!" Gleicher broke in with feeling.

It was one of the first affairs for which he had been made responsible after transferring to the *Abwehr*. He had only just had time to look into the case and draw up his plans when the Gestapo intervened with their usual brutality.

"Those Gestapo swine sabotaged my work completely. If we'd waited another fortnight we should have had the whole lot in the bag, whereas all they got was the small fry."

"They're always in too much of a hurry," Otto agreed.

Otto unreservedly shared his chief's feelings on this

point. The spirit of hostile rivalry between the *Abwehr* and the Gestapo was apparent to every member of both organizations and sometimes resulted in their jeopardizing the efficacy of the common struggle against Allied spies.

"And yet," he went on, pursing his lips, "they got some results on that occasion."

"What results?" Gleicher protested. "A few subordinates arrested; some poor bloody fools wiped out who wanted to destroy three old locomotives and that's all."

"Not very important people, it's true," Otto conceded. "Nevertheless, about fifty of the enemy liquidated. . . ."

"And the means employed to attain this brilliant success?" Gleicher demanded. To him the men of the Gestapo were odious for a number of reasons. He had espoused the cause of the rival organization; he hated the secret police instinctively; and he had been reprimanded at a high level for letting them steal a march on him. "The means? Torture. That's all they know. Take away their blackjacks, their electric-shock machines, and the rest of their repulsive contraptions, and they're incapable of obtaining the slightest information. I, on the other hand, as I've said before, Otto, would have nabbed the whole lot, and without grilling the soles of anyone's feet, as they did, apparently."

"I'm sure you would have, Herr Doktor. Please don't think I'm trying to stand up for them; although, in certain circumstances, brutality. . . ."

His reticence showed that even though he hated the Gestapo at least as much as his chief, he was not absolutely opposed on principle to some of its methods.

Colonel von Gleicher, who felt deeply on this subject, declared in a biting tone:

"I tell you, Otto, those practices are not only dishonorable but stupid. When you think in those terms, you're incapable of proper planning and find yourself hoodwinked by the first fool you come across who invents some cock-and-bull story for fear of being maltreated. No one is going to use torture in this service as long as I have the honor of directing it. *Der Nachtrichtendienst ist ein Herrendienst,** and don't forget it."

Otto acquiesced, as he always did when his chief quoted this particular phrase attributed to Admiral Canaris—which he was apt to do at least once a week. Gleicher continued:

"Just look at their stupidity. In the case of the Lachaume farm, they were clumsy enough to let the principal character and his radio operator escape before getting all they knew out of them, simply because they were impatient to make some spectacular arrests and have a good laugh at our expense."

"That's not altogether accurate, Herr Doktor. One of the two men, Cousin, it is true, did get away. The other, the radio operator, died."

"Does that make it any better? So he died, did he? That's even more stupid. The result of their treatment, I suppose?"

"They deny it, Herr Doktor, but it's more than likely."

Gleicher raised his eyes to the ceiling and heaved a sigh.

"Oh, well . . . Go on with your story."

* Intelligence work is a noble profession—an occupation for gentlemen.

"To get back to that business . . . did you know, Herr Doktor, that the Gestapo officer and his second-in-command were killed that night during the ambush they had set for the raiding party? In spite of being surprised, the saboteurs put up a stiff fight before being wiped out."

"I didn't know, but I can't say I'm terribly sorry."

"Since the two henchmen who stayed behind at the farm to guard the prisoners were also killed, there seems to be no living witness to the revelations made by one of the men."

"Imbeciles," Gleicher muttered.

"Not entirely, at least not in this case, Herr Doktor, for the man's confession was taken down on a tape recorder, and the tape has been found intact. Cousin failed to destroy it when he made his getaway; perhaps he didn't know the machine was there."

"And this tape?"

"Was examined carefully, of course, by the Gestapo, and all the information followed up some time ago. It's now filed away in the archives."

Gleicher peered at his assistant intently.

"How do you know all this, Otto?"

"I planted an agent among those gentlemen," Otto admitted. "It has proved quite useful at times."

Colonel Count von Gleicher eyed him with disdain, unwilling to approve of this underhand spying on a rival service. He also resented the fact that his subordinate should have acted on his initiative without first consulting him. He did not remonstrate with him, however, considering, on second thought, that these practices, which perhaps were very useful, should remain unknown to the lords of the profession.

"My agent," Otto added casually, "has undertaken to get hold of this document and hand it over to us. He'll have to be paid, of course."

"What good is it to us? And, besides, what has it got to do with the business we're engaged on at the moment?"

Otto spoke slowly, with a certain emphasis, anxious to make the most of what he had to say.

"The identification section," he observed, "believes that Cousin and Arvers may be one and the same person. They even think it's more than likely."

Gleicher could not help betraying his surprise by giving a faint whistle.

"But we are more or less certain, aren't we, that Arvers was dropped with his wife only a short time ago?"

"We are also almost certain that the other man succeeded in getting back to England. They've unearthed an old photograph of Cousin. It's the only one they've got and it isn't very clear, but after comparing it with Arvers', the experts are almost certain. Here they are, anyway."

Gleicher bent over them. It was he himself who had managed to take a snapshot of Arvers, without his knowing it, from the garden of his villa. He had not wished to risk arousing suspicion by entrusting one of his agents with this task. He was also anxious to acquaint himself with the humblest duties of his new profession, and this detective-story procedure amused him. He looked at the two prints for a long time. He had never seen Cousin, even though he had had some dealings with his network.

"There's a vague resemblance, perhaps, but there are many points that don't agree at all."

"Just the ones it would be easy to modify, Herr Doktor—the haircut, the spectacles, the mustache . . ."

"But you haven't answered my first question yet. What is the use of the tape if all the information has already been exploited?"

"I wasn't thinking of the *contents* of the tape, Herr Doktor."

"Well, then," said Gleicher, who felt considerably put out by his subordinate's mysterious manner, "tell me how the confessions of his former radio operator can be of any help in my dealings with Arvers."

"If that's what really happened—I mean the official version: the man under torture finally talked, what could be more natural?—then this document won't be of any help, of course. Only . . ."

"Only what?"

"There's another possibility," said Otto. "When my agent saw I was interested in the case, he obtained further details for me. It was believed that all witnesses to the interrogation had been killed. But one has been found—a rather simple-minded strong-arm man who had never given his opinion because no one had ever asked him for it. He actually helped to *interrogate* the radio operator. Now, on this point he is absolutely adamant—the man never talked."

Gleicher suppressed an exclamation and merely emitted another whistle of surprise. Otto fell silent for a moment, to allow time for his chief's mind to come to a certain conclusion, then went on:

"Of course, I can't vouch for the truth of this. Allowances have to be made for this fellow's personality—an absolute brute of a man. But why shouldn't he have retained a perfectly clear recollection of that scene?"

"And yet he came back?" muttered Gleicher, who was following his own train of thought.

"Rather strange, on the face of it, but it can probably be explained."

"How much is your agent asking for the tape?" Gleicher asked after a moment's reflection.

Otto mentioned a fairly steep price. Gleicher brought his fist down on the table.

"Buy it, Otto! Go and buy it right away and don't waste any time bargaining. Do you think you can get hold of it within the next half hour?"

"Out of the question, Herr Doktor. It will take me at least a day or two."

"Never mind . . . though I should have liked to hear it played through before going down there this evening. . . ."

He got up, put on his spectacles again, and set about resuming his bourgeois aspect.

"Good work, Otto," he said as he left the office. "You may rest assured that I shall listen to every intonation of his voice with the utmost attention."

18   In the living room of the villa, Arvers was moodily contemplating a message that had just come in from London. Claire was reading in a corner of the room—or was she only pretending to be reading? Her most commonplace occupations struck him as being pretexts for spying on him, and he controlled the muscles of his face so as not to reveal a clue to his feelings.

The message was fairly long and contained nothing of particular interest, but he was irritated to detect throughout its contents a certain lack of appreciation of his work—no specific complaint, but a sort of unexpressed regret that his activity was not more fruitful. The message acknowledged receipt of the documents that had arrived by the previous mails and especially the information sent a few days earlier by Claire, after Gleicher's last visit. Not only did it not contain a single word of encouragement, such as: "Continue with the good work," as often used to happen, but it was scattered with remarks of this sort: "Could be useful at a pinch," and "This has been known to us for some time," and even "Much more urgent to give details on such-and-such a point, the importance of which seems to escape you. More difficult, certainly, but it should be possible if reasonable risks are taken."

He was cut to the quick by the sarcastic tone of this last remark. This was not characteristic of Austin, who generally drafted the messages. Some big shot, comfortably ensconced in his armchair, had probably wanted to add his grain of salt and show his authority. Arvers read it through again. There was no doubt about it: they were insinuating that he was not doing his best. Was it his fault that his role was so restricted and that he depended entirely on Gleicher for the information he provided? If the German was making a fool of them, he, Arvers, could hardly be blamed; all he could do was express his dissatisfaction.

Not that he ever failed to do so. The recollection of his last meeting with Gleicher did something to soothe his injured pride. Since the traitor had appeared rather resentful of his usual tone of authority, he had given him a thorough dressing-down, like a schoolboy, and intimated that he held the German's honor and even his life in the palm of his hand—a statement from which he derived a singular pleasure. Gleicher had quickly resumed his humble attitude and promised to do his utmost to fulfill his demands. . . . Yet the last batch of information was worthless, or almost so, according to London! He made a note to take Gleicher down a peg in the course of their next meeting. Meanwhile, he himself was the scapegoat. He was the one whom his superiors appeared to consider too timid—even pusillanimous, perhaps?

Pusillanimous! He became red in the face and could not suppress a gesture of anger. He regretted this at once, sensing that this movement had not escaped Claire and that she had raised her head. His whole body had become extraordinarily sensitive to Claire's gaze. He glanced in her direction. He was not mistaken: she was peering at him over the edge of her book. He became even redder as he tried to explain his attitude.

"It's this message," he muttered irritably. "They really seem to think we're just twiddling our thumbs. They don't realize the conditions in which one has to work when engaged in clandestine activity."

His voice sounded false and he knew it. Claire knew as well as he did that London was fully aware of the difficulties confronting secret agents. Nor did it escape her that his present job entailed infinitely less danger than many other missions. He felt the need of justifying himself still further in the eyes of this girl, whose silence was, as usual, filled with malevolence.

"If we don't take great risks, it's only in order to abide by their instructions."

The "we" was a tentative effort to create a team spirit between them. He often endeavored by such means to break through the constraint and distrust that made their relationship intolerable. It had never led to any result. With a similar intention, while walking arm in arm through the countryside, as they often did to fulfill the demands of their roles, so as to be noticed by the local peasants, he had even dared, at the beginning, to make a joke of their status as a young married couple and to hold her more tightly than was strictly necessary. He did this without any ulterior motive, simply to introduce a little humanity into their relationship, but she had glared at him with such disdain that he had quickly given up these familiarities.

"Anyway, darling, I don't see what more we can do in this hole they've put us in."

He sometimes called her "darling" even when they were alone together. His excuse was that he did not want to lose the habit; in fact, it was only because the word seemed to decrease the hostility of her presence. Today he was persisting in his efforts to conciliate her and doing his utmost to win her approval.

Claire said nothing in reply but allowed a faint smile to appear on her lips—her way of expressing her scornful pity and contempt, which made him tremble with anger and burn with a wild desire to show her how completely mistaken she was about him.

He sincerely regretted what he had just said, for her smile was quite plain: it meant that she, at any rate, saw quite clearly what more they could do. Without saying a word, as though he was unworthy of a fuller explanation, she thereby reminded him of an extraordinary conversation they had had the day before.

A distant cousin of Claire's, who worked at an inn in the depths of the forest a few miles away, had given her some valuable information without himself being aware of its importance. The inn had been requisitioned for three days because a certain Herr Müller wanted to go down there for a short rest. Müller was not his real name; Claire's cousin had discovered this, during one of Herr Müller's previous visits, from a member of his retinue who spoke French. The mystery man was none other than Dr. Bergen, a person of considerable status. Claire and Arvers were well aware of his importance, for Bergen had long ago been identified by the Allied services as one of the greatest authorities on secret weapons. They also knew he came to the coast at regular intervals and spent a few days there.

Claire had shed her usual reserve as she reported this conversation. Some networks would have paid a high price for the information her cousin had given her without having the remotest idea of her undercover activity.

"He's arriving tomorrow. He'll be staying three days, and his habits are well known. He works in his room all afternoon and goes for a long walk in the forest every morning. At the inn the rooms next to his are occupied by a secretary and four men in civilian clothes, probably policemen. He doesn't seem to care for the latter's company, and they never accompany him on his walks. For their part, his bodyguards appear to treat these visits as a holiday. Their activity is limited to searching the house and reconnoitering the immediate surroundings when they first arrive. In the evenings, whereas Bergen goes to bed early, they stay up drinking until all hours and get up extremely late. Bergen goes out very early, alone. I know every inch of the forest. I often used to go there as a child. We'll never have such an opportunity again."

She had fallen silent, studying his reactions as usual. Then she had pointedly added:

"Bergen's a weedy little chap and never carries a gun."

At first he had pretended not to understand her implicit suggestion and had merely said:

"We'll have to notify London immediately."

"It's much too late for them to do anything. He's arriving tomorrow."

"Then it will have to wait for the next time. See that your cousin gives you sufficient warning."

"An opportunity like this doesn't occur every day. We must snap it up and thank our lucky stars. . . . I tell you, I know the forest like the back of my hand. He always takes the same path."

Once again she had looked at him intently, and he fancied he already saw that odious smile on her lips. It was no longer possible for him to pretend that he had not grasped her meaning. Realizing he would have to give some explanation for his passive attitude, he tried to conceal his embarrassment under an almost paternal air of authority.

"I must remind you, darling, that one of the first rules of any secret service is to keep intelligence apart from action. We're condemned, alas, to intelligence. I can understand how you feel at missing such an opportunity. Don't imagine I'm not equally disappointed. If only . . . But no, it's no use," he concluded, pretending to reconsider his decision; "we haven't the right to take action on our own."

He had felt at once that she looked upon these excellent reasons of his as weak excuses. Admittedly, his voice had not been very convincing. And now, at this moment, under Claire's scornful gaze, he realized this conversation had been preying on his mind ever since the previous day.

She still did not reply to his remark: "I can't see what more we can do," but her smile became more pronounced and frankly sarcastic. He averted his gaze, unable to support this calculated insult any longer. His eyes fell on the message from London, which seemed to reflect contempt of a slightly more subtle kind but similar to the scorn she was pouring on him. The violence of his shame and rage made him tremble and fired him with an irresistible urge—the brutal reaction of his pride against the monstrous injustice of ignominious suspicions.

"So that's how it is, is it?" he exclaimed, bringing his clenched fist down on the table. "They think we're being overcautious, is that it? Well, they'll soon see. We're going to take action for a change."

19   He had no control over these words at
the moment he uttered them. It was only in the silence
that followed his declaration that he realized he had
unleashed a fatal chain of events, culminating for him
in a fresh ordeal that gave him a vague presentiment of
horror. He cursed himself for having once again become his own executioner, but the change in Claire's
attitude prolonged the intoxication of his hasty decision.

She looked at him in amazement and disbelief. The
smile had frozen on her face. He derived such solace
from her manifest stupefaction that he continued to
pursue the course on which he had blindly embarked,
burning his boats, taking a keen pleasure in disclosing
his plans by slow degrees, in order to enjoy her discom-

fiture the more. He now spoke solemnly, deliberately, weighing every word as he was drawn deeper and deeper into the mesh.

"Bergen's still got two more days at the inn?"

"Tomorrow and the day after."

"And he goes for his walk all by himself?"

"All by himself."

"You say you know the forest pretty well?"

"Every tree, every bush, every rock."

"How long does it take to get there?"

"Less than two hours. There are several shortcuts."

He could no longer avoid the outcome. He paused for a moment; then, with the cool determination of a leader weighing all the risks, declared briskly:

"Very well, then. If you'll agree to come with me, I'll see to him."

He was delighted to see her bite her lip with anger, and this sight was all he needed to appease his anguish. She, in turn, now began to raise objections, and her voice was trembling.

"But you said we ought to confine ourselves to intelligence."

"In principle, yes. But the opportunity's too good to miss."

"We risk being censured by London."

"Almost certainly," he said in a tone of calm defiance. "That's just another risk we'll have to take. But there's one thing that takes precedence over everything else, darling. I've thought about it very seriously—the existence of this fellow Bergen is a menace to thousands, possibly millions, of human lives. There's no getting away from that. In a case like this, the ends justify a divergence from our principles. I'll take all the responsibility . . . But, of course, if you don't like the idea, I can't force you to cooperate."

He was allowing himself the supreme satisfaction of showing that he now suspected her of lack of courage. She merely shrugged her shoulders.

"I'll show you how to get there. If we leave tonight we'll be there before daybreak."

"Tonight!"

His voice betrayed the terror he suddenly felt. He had not thought of acting so soon. In his own mind he had vaguely decided on the day after tomorrow, and this forty-eight hours' deferment had helped to soften the harsh reality.

"Tonight."

Their dialogue resembled a duel between two expert swordsmen. As she suddenly fixed her eyes on him, deriving fresh hope from his dismay, he parried her thrust automatically.

"Right. We'll leave tonight so as to be in position by daybreak. We musn't let this opportunity slip through our fingers. Then, if anything goes wrong tomorrow, we'll still have another day."

They fell silent. He was hoping she would acknowledge his audacity with at least a word or two of commendation but, having recovered from her surprise, she now seemed to be absorbed in her own thoughts. He waited anxiously for the outcome of this inner deliberation.

"How are you going to kill him, darling?" she finally asked.

He could see she was preparing a counterattack. Her

gentle, insidious tone and the "darling," which she herself never used in private, were enough to reveal her intention. The word "kill" almost made him jump out of his skin. He managed, however, to retain an appearance of composure.

"I'll take one of the revolvers that are hidden in your mother's house."

"But you don't seem to realize . . . It'll have to be done in silence."

Each word was charged with a special ferocity. She went on methodically, as though explaining a theorem to a child.

"The shots couldn't fail to be heard, not only by his bodyguard but also by the French police post that is hardly any distance away. Although the forest is fairly dense in the neighborhood of the inn, it doesn't stretch very far. They'd be bound to find us. No, that's out of the question."

She pretended to turn the matter over in her mind, like an eager colleague who was trying to work out for him the best solution to a tricky problem.

"Cut his throat? Perhaps. But you told me that requires a perfect and rather difficult technique. Let's see, now . . . I think," she concluded, looking him straight in the eyes, "I think this would be an ideal opportunity to use your piano wire."

He broke out into a cold sweat and at the same time felt a violent urge to strangle her rather than anyone else. He was the one—as usual—who had first brought up the question of piano wire: in London, when they were assembling their operational kit.

"It's worth taking a few lengths with us," he had

said. "You can't always find what you want on the spot just when you happen to need it."

Flaunting his experience, he had then told her what he had learned in his special training course—according to some experts, strangling was the easiest and surest method of getting rid of an enemy in silence; the use of a knife required too much practice.

This was an obvious occasion for using piano wire; she was right. But in her suggestion he detected the devilish urge to test him to the utmost limit by multiplying the dangers of the task he had set himself in a moment of madness. "Strangling," "stabbing"—these words caused him no concern in a training camp in England, so remote and improbable appeared the act they represented. Here, today, when it was a question of a few hours, the terms assumed a very different aspect.

He was caught in a trap. He could not think of a single valid objection to the terrible logic of her conclusion: a pistol shot was clearly unwise. It had to be the piano wire, which he himself had praised and which he had insisted on bringing along, in the event of circumstances of this very kind. At a pinch, he could still choose between this method and a knife, but he would have to make up his mind immediately; he could not stand the torment of her gaze a moment longer. She required an immediate reply and could scarcely wait to inflict that smile of hers on him again.

"I choose the wire," he said in a flat voice.

From his mode of expression, one might have supposed he himself was the intended victim. He realized this and corrected himself, managing to assume a steadier tone in a heroic attempt to correct the ambiguous turn of phrase from which his merciless companion might be able to divine his pitiful state of mind.

"You're right, darling, it's the surest method. I'll jump on him from behind and strangle him. He won't have time to utter a sound."

20　　　　"He couldn't bring himself to do it. At the last moment he suddenly lost his nerve and collapsed like a pricked balloon. Thank heavens! If he had managed to bring it off, I think I should have given up the struggle. He was compelled to show his cowardice, but he did not admit it."

In front of her mother, Claire forced herself to assume an exultant tone. As a matter of fact, she was at the end of her rope. The constant battle she waged against Arvers was beginning to wear her down as much as him. She did her best to look upon her adversary's failure as a victory, whereas it was nothing more than a point in her favor after a long series of setbacks.

"Tell me about it."

The old woman retained her usual self-possession. It would have needed a great deal more than an abortive attempt on the life of a German to crush her spirit. She still had the same sullen, stubborn, obdurate expression that nothing could alter except, perhaps, the fulfillment of her highest hope—a hope that had gradually turned her features into a strained and frozen mask.

Claire had just arrived, out of breath, overwrought, and on the point of collapse. Her mother seemed annoyed to see her displaying such lack of self-control, and she scarcely seemed to give a thought to the danger her daughter had courted. She poured out a drink for her and repeated gruffly:

"Tell me about it."

Claire took a deep breath and managed to master her feelings sufficiently to embark on her story. The previous evening, she had told her mother about the scheme Arvers had in mind. She reported their enemy's gestures and actions to her every day, conscientiously listening in return to her advice, or, rather, her orders.

"We set out after dark. He hadn't eaten anything all evening and had locked himself in his room earlier. I managed to get quite close to him before leaving the villa. It wasn't too easy; he obstinately kept moving away. He smelled of liquor."

"He smelled of liquor," her mother echoed with satisfaction.

She made a mental note of every detail of Arvers' behavior, no matter how trivial. These she mentally pieced together to form a sort of file that grew larger each day, and which she thought would finally burst open someday, revealing the truth.

"He smelled of liquor even though he had taken the precaution of cleaning his teeth. I heard him. He must have spent most of the evening at the bottle. We walked down the road in silence, then I led the way along the shortcuts. I could hear him gasping for breath just behind me. He could hardly keep up. I went on walking as fast as I could."

"Good," her mother observed with satisfaction.

"Several times he asked me to slow down a little, ostensibly because of the darkness. Once he asked me in a hoarse voice to stop. He put his hand to his heart. He was on his last legs. I shone my flashlight in his face. He looked so ghastly that even I was terrified and took a step backward. If he had had the strength or the courage, it's me he would have killed."

"But he hasn't got the strength or the courage."

"I know. That's what reassured me a little. We started off again. We arrived close to the inn at daybreak. I had no difficulty in finding the spot I had thought of as the most suitable for an ambush—a dense thicket, traversed by the path leading from the house. Bergen was bound to come that way. Close by there are some outcrops of rock overlooking the wood and affording a view of the front of the house. We climbed to the top of one of them, after preparing a hide-out down below. He followed me like an automaton and kept shivering all the time."

"Shivering," her mother echoed.

"He flopped down on the ground, no longer capable of assuming a bold front. I felt he was on the point of collapse. I had never seen him in such a pitiful condition. His lips moved as though he wanted to say something, and he looked at me imploringly. I thought— yes, for several seconds I thought he was going to make a clean breast of everything. He was lying slightly on one side, his hand to his chest and trembling from head to foot."

"Go on," her mother exclaimed impatiently, without sharing the emotion her daughter felt at the recollection of this scene.

"Then he pulled himself together . . ."

Her mother broke in severely:

"You should have harried him, pressed home your advantage."

"I didn't have time to. He recovered his self-possession as the sun began to rise over the forest. He managed to sit up again. I could see he was making a desperate effort. He began keeping a close watch on the inn. The front door swung open and Bergen came out, alone. I had had him described to me—a wizened little man with short, stumpy legs. It was he, all right. He went through the garden and disappeared into the wood. In less than ten minutes he would be right below us. We just had time to climb down from our observation post, then we hid behind a bush on the edge of the path. He was bound to pass less than six feet away."

"What was Arvers' behavior like at that stage?"

"It struck me as rather strange. Whereas he was almost fainting five minutes before, he now seemed quite calm and almost determined. He took the wire out of his pocket and stretched it in his hands as though to test its strength. But I'm sure—in fact, I realized later—that he had already made up his mind not to go through with it. This show of determination was sheer pretense. All he was thinking of was the excuse he would have to give me."

"I'm sure you're right."

"But at that moment he looked like a new man, and I wondered if he might not really see the thing through."

"No chance of that!" her mother muttered. "I can see it all as clearly as though I had been there myself."

"It was only when I heard Bergen's footsteps approaching that I saw through his little game. At this point his expression changed and he tapped his forehead as though a sudden thought had just flashed through his mind. All this was only designed to cloak his insufficiency.

"When he saw Bergen fifty yards off, he seized me by the arm. I tried to slip away, but he got a firmer grip on me, knocked me over, lay down on top of me so as to pin me to the ground, and whispered in my ear: 'Whatever you do, don't move. It has only just struck me. We mustn't. It's impossible.'

"I was wild with anger. I felt like jumping up and pouncing on the German myself, just to see what he would do."

"Why didn't you?"

"I couldn't. He was pressing down on me with all his weight, and his hand was clamped over my mouth. Bergen went by, walking very quickly, without being aware of our presence.

"He waited for some time before releasing me. When he was sure the German was out of earshot he spoke to me under his breath, assuming an air of assurance that infuriated me.

"'It would have been sheer lunacy,' he said. 'Our eagerness made us lose our heads. Think of the reprisals such an incident would provoke throughout the whole district.'

" 'I thought you had weighed all the risks,' I retorted. 'Bergen's existence endangers thousands, possibly millions, of human lives.'

"Those were the very words he had used. His face turned scarlet. He looked slightly put out for a moment, but went on vehemently:

" 'It doesn't matter about us. We don't count. We've already staked our lives. But do you realize the Germans would shoot half the people in your village, which happens to be the nearest one? And have you thought about your mother?"

"This was obviously just an excuse. Even so, all the scorn I managed to put into my expression did nothing to alter the situation. He still managed to get away with it."

"We'll get him someday," her mother said. "After all, it's a setback for him. He must have realized you saw through him."

"Naturally. On our way back he could hardly bring himself to look at me."

"We'll get him," her mother repeated, nodding her head. "The next time you mustn't let him recover his self-possession. I know what he's like now. He's the sort of man you have to harry. He'll always get away with it if you give him time to think."

21   Arvers was waiting for Gleicher, who had arrived at the villa at dusk and was to come over and join him after dinner. He tried to shake off the image of Bergen in the wood and the bitter taste left by the memory of his failure. He succeeded by concentrating on the reception he was preparing for the traitor and by repeating under his breath the orders he was going to give him. In the gloomy atmosphere in which he was struggling, Gleicher's visits came like rays of sunshine.

The German knocked gently on the door at the appointed hour and appeared in the guise in which Arvers knew him, interweaving into his bourgeois manner a variety of facial contortions designed to express servility, greed, and fear. Arvers did not even invite him to sit down. With his hands in his pockets and a forbidding expression on his face that, to his intense delight, forced his victim to bow his head, he harshly listed his complaints. Claire was on the other side of the room, separated from them by a half-open movable partition. He spoke fairly loudly so that she should not miss a single word of his tirade.

"I may as well tell you, my good man, that I'm far from satisfied with your work. The last batch of information I bought from you was utterly worthless. I thought so at the time, and my service has since confirmed it. At the rate I pay you, I think I can expect something better than that sort of trash."

He shifted his position slightly to see what Claire was doing. She was busy writing and looked as though she had not heard a word. He was vexed by this but derived some consolation from the manifest discomfiture of Gleicher, who was timidly mumbling some lame excuse. Arvers interrupted with a withering gesture to show he had not yet finished with him.

"I'd like to point out that up to now I've been scrupulously fair in my dealings with you. If you can't be a little more conscientious yourself, I'll have to make other arrangements."

He felt intoxicated by the sound of his own words. Claire stopped writing and made an abrupt gesture, which his pride interpreted as a sign of approval, whereas in fact it expressed only the girl's annoyance at his attitude. He went on, striving to create an effect by way of contrast, switching straight to a mysterious, almost sinister tone.

"Not to mention, of course, the extremely serious steps that I shan't hesitate to take in order to ensure your discretion."

This was the way to handle a traitor! The fellow was entirely at his mercy. He had seen through him com-

pletely. He was not only corrupt but also contempt-
ible—the very thought of him made Arvers feel sick.
To realize what sort of man he was, you only had to
look at him now—cringing instead of standing up to
him. Arvers interrupted him again in a furious tone:

"That'll be all for the moment. But don't say I didn't
warn you. Now then, what have you brought me today?"

The German opened his brief case and handed him
some papers that Arvers began studying, shrugging his
shoulders from time to time. Gleicher watched him
closely and seemed lost in thought. His reflections must
have been sufficiently absorbing to make him gradually
abandon his servile manner. In the end he decided to
speak, in a voice still deferential but at the same time
filled with a subtle, almost imperceptible undertone
that would have escaped anyone but Arvers, who was
acutely sensitive to these fine distinctions.

"Herr Arvers," Gleicher was saying, "I owe you an
apology. I'm ashamed of myself, positively ashamed.
You're absolutely right: that last lot of information
wasn't worthy of you."

Arvers' peculiar sense was immediately alerted. He
detected a note of irony in this suspicious display of
humility. It was so unexpected that he felt a dull shock
and shivered as though it were a portent of danger.
Since his return to France, any surprise he suffered was
invariably accompanied by a vague foreboding. He
glanced automatically in Claire's direction, anxious to
see whether she, too, had been struck by these unusual
inflections; but she had resumed her work and appeared
not to have noticed.

"You're absolutely right, Herr Arvers, that last lot
of information wasn't worthy of you, and I'm afraid

this batch isn't particularly important, either. Believe me, it's not my fault; after all, I had a great deal of difficulty getting it. But I'm anxious to give value for the money I earn and I'd like to prove this to you. Do you realize, Herr Arvers, that even before you voiced your complaints—which are justified, absolutely justified—my conscience was pricking me? Honestly, I've felt deep remorse at having failed to deliver the goods these last few weeks.

"I've done my utmost to redeem myself, and I think I've succeeded. Yes, at last I'm in a position to let you have a document of exceptional value, a document worthy of you, Herr Arvers—and also of myself, for I, too, have my pride."

He began to reveal his heavy guns. This moment was his reward for a long period of mortification, during which he had been forced to play a loathsome role.

"And where's this marvelous document of yours?" Arvers asked, making an effort to recover his air of authority. "All I see here is the usual drivel."

"I didn't bring it with me. It belongs to a friend of mine who would probably let me have it; but he is fully aware of its value. He's asking an extremely steep price, Herr Arvers."

"How can I tell if it's really worth anything or not?"

Gleicher lowered his voice so as not to be overheard and whispered in a mysterious manner:

"You can listen to it this evening, Herr Arvers. It's in my villa."

"Listen to it?"

"Yes. It isn't a piece of paper, it's a tape recording."

Arvers gave a start. At the sound of the words "tape recording," which suggested no specific danger, the feeling of apprehension caused by his visitor's behavior intensified. He had the uneasy suspicion that this new material furnished an alarming explanation of the apparent insignificance of some incident—one he had forgotten long before, because of its unimportance, and that he could not yet call to mind exactly. Perhaps the truth was already beginning to emerge in his subconscious by the usual tortuous paths—paths more akin to premonition than to rational knowledge.

"A tape recording," he echoed, also lowering his voice so that Claire could not hear.

"A tape recording. When you've heard it, I'm sure you'll appreciate its importance as I do—and also," Gleicher added with a wink, "its extremely confidential character, Herr Arvers. This document must not be divulged to any subordinate. That's why I didn't bring it here. But if you'd be so kind as to come around to my place—it's only a step, Herr Arvers—you'll be able to see for yourself immediately."

It was no longer possible to be mistaken about his attitude. This was irony—ponderous, German irony.

Arvers made yet another attempt to master his feelings and recover his position by haughtily declaring it was probably nothing but the usual trash, for which it was scarcely worth his while to go to so much trouble. Gleicher then told him he would be well advised to take the trouble; his manner was suddenly so solemn that Arvers once again felt he was losing ground. His mental anguish had become so intense that he could not bring himself to ask for further details about the mysterious tape.

Yet he still could not make up his mind. He had already been to Gleicher's villa. Until now he had not been afraid of the possibility of foul play on Gleicher's part, believing the man to be too compromised to be able to do him any harm; but this evening his manner was distinctly alarming. The German read his thoughts.

"Believe me, Herr Arvers, you have nothing to fear. I give you my word, this isn't a trap."

"I'm not afraid of you," Arvers replied sharply. "Let's be off."

They went out into the dark. Gleicher led the way without saying a word and Arvers asked no questions. This traitor, whom he thought he held in the palm of his hand, was beginning to appear a formidable person, an enemy to be added to the long list of those who were bent on disturbing the harmonious development of his dreams.

Gleicher showed him into the living room, which was brightly lit. Arvers gave a start as he saw there was someone there already. Otto rose to his feet as they came in.

"Gently, now, Herr Arvers," Gleicher chuckled. "You're very jumpy, aren't you? It's only Otto, the friend I was telling you about. He has known about you for a long time. He wanted to meet you in person. You can trust him completely. He knows whom he's dealing with . . . don't you, Otto?"

Otto nodded, grinning at his chief's playful remark. Gleicher seemed extremely pleased with himself and poured drinks for them.

"Herr Arvers is in rather a hurry, Otto," he went on. "We mustn't waste his precious time. We'd better start our little audition right away. Are you ready, Herr Arvers?"

Arvers acquiesced with a gesture. Otto went over

and switched on the tape recorder he had brought in and placed in a corner of the room. Then he straightened up and remained standing by the machine, watching Arvers intently. All they could hear at first were a few indistinct sounds.

"Listen carefully, Herr Arvers," Gleicher repeated. "It's a really remarkable recording."

22   At first Arvers did not understand at all. He failed to recognize his own voice. For a few seconds he thought he was listening to a stranger talking and felt a momentary sense of relief—but only for a few seconds, as though some perverse power had decided to grant him this brief respite so that the blow it dealt him later should be all the more crushing.

Then, with the gradual progression of a refined torture, while his heart began to thunder and the walls of his palace of illusions started to crumble about his ears, he felt himself sinking into a bottomless pit of disaster by sufficiently slow degrees for his conscious mind to grasp every detail of this utter hell.

A dismal swarm of gruesome memories, which the miraculous will of a mind bent on self-preservation had warded off for several months, now started circling around him, approaching more closely at each successive revolution, spinning faster and faster, drawing nearer and nearer to a certain central image, the axis of their rotation—a human shape none other than himself, bound hand and foot, lying powerless on a heap of straw in a room in a tumble-down farmhouse.

Faster and faster, in time with the accelerated rhythm of his heart, the demons of reality, released from the dark cage in which he had kept them imprisoned, started to smother him under their loathsome wings, whispering in his ear in a conspiratorial tone, murmuring one after another their scraps of partial evidence, then raising the pitch and hastening the pace of their monstrous accusations until their yelps dissolved into a single prolonged shriek. This clamor brought to life a former state of being that, in spite of the sublime crusade of oblivion waged by his mind, had existed at some point in the past, leaving its mark in the indelible archives of time and space. Bit by bit this state emerged from the mists in which he had hidden it away, his ignominy intensifying at each revolution of the tape. The words now came back to him like long-lost friends. They were so familiar that he moved his lips and involuntarily uttered them at the same time as the machine—sometimes even a split second before—unconsciously allowing his present voice to serve as an accompaniment to this sinister echo from the past.

When Cousin had dared to open his eyes again, the Gestapo officer had his back turned toward him and was bending over an instrument Cousin had never seen before, which was connected by some wires to a dry-cell battery. He thought it might be a generator, clutching at the wild hope that he was simply going to be subjected to a few electric shocks—how gentle that torture now seemed!—but it wasn't that at all. The officer looked around, abandoned the mysterious machine, and signaled to one of his men. The man walked over toward Cousin brandishing the poker, the point of which was glowing as brightly as a star.

That was the precise moment he had given in—at the mere sight of the red-hot iron. He could not bear the idea of its contact with his flesh. He was overwhelmed by the anticipation of the pain. He surrendered in a flash, in wild haste born of headlong panic. Up till then he had somehow hoped to gain a little time by arguing with his executioners. These vague intentions were instantly obliterated by the gleam of the poker.

There was only one thought left in his head, only one desire onto which his mind could fasten—to be quick about it, so as not to give the man time to take another step. His dominating terror now was that he might not be able to talk soon enough, that at the last moment—just when there was nothing he would refuse them—he might not be able to make them understand, that he might not have time to convince them he was at their mercy, body and soul, only too ready to do whatever they asked. Provided they had no doubt on that score! Provided they did not think they would need to break down his resistance by a brief application of the iron!

And so, with his brain inflamed by the urgency of his surrender, he succeeded, in the time it took for the man to take one step forward, in spitting out his glass capsule—the poison he had never had any intention of swallowing—and in blurting out these words, words the tape was now playing back to him with relentless fidelity:

"Stop, stop! I'll talk! I'll tell you everything, everything! I'll do whatever you wish! The whole network . . . the links with London . . . names and addresses, I'll give you the whole thing."

With cruel perfection the machine reproduced all the fine nuances of his terror—his stumbling speech, for instance, when he almost choked, so thickly did the words gather in his throat, so anxious was he to furnish immediately as much information as possible.

Since the Gestapo officer appeared to hesitate, he had hastened to repeat his offer.

"It's extremely urgent . . . As you see, I'm not trying to hide anything . . . Tonight, this evening . . . No time to lose . . . A raid organized . . . The roundhouse . . . A party of twenty . . . Rendezvous at the Café du Commerce . . . I can give you the address . . . The recognition signal is . . ."

His abject terror came over with surprising clarity. There was no need for him to mention this operation—no need, except, perhaps, the urgency to make it quite plain to them that torture was superfluous. He insisted on making this gratuitous confession because he felt it was the best proof of his readiness to fall in with their wishes.

"Tonight . . . In a few hours; you'll just barely have time . . . Twenty men . . . At the Café du Commerce. There are some submachine guns hidden away there . . . Also some explosives."

The executioner had halted at a signal from his chief. Even after this longed-for reprieve was granted, Cousin went on groveling, begging for mercy, blurting out the first thing that came into his head in order to ingratiate himself with them.

"Don't hurt me. There's no need for that. I can be extremely useful to you. I have the confidence of my superiors. Think how helpful I can be to you . . ."

The recording went on in this vein for several minutes, punctuated by questions from the Gestapo officer, to which Cousin replied with painstaking accuracy, over and above what was demanded of him. This practical demonstration of his cowardice caused him untold agony. He felt he could not stand it a moment longer. This torture had to be brought to an end one way or another. He was certainly going to faint. But the loss of consciousness for which he prayed with all his might was denied him and he had to listen to the bitter end, unable even to summon up sufficient strength to cover his ears with his hands.

The audition was over. Otto had switched off the machine some time before and was now waiting, motionless, for an order from his chief, who seemed to be in no particular hurry. Gleicher had listened to the tape several times before, but each time it gave him fresh food for thought. He emerged abruptly from his daydream to straighten his back, pull in his stomach, and assume the demeanor of Colonel Count von Gleicher. It was an unconscious reaction of defense against the servility of the person slumped in the armchair, in front of whom he felt it unworthy to force himself to keep up his former role.

"Give him a drink, Otto," he said contemptuously, "otherwise he'll pass out on us and that wouldn't do at all. . . . Well, my dear sir, now you've heard what we had to tell you. I don't intend to make any comment. But when you've pulled yourself together a little, I'll tell you exactly what I want from you."

His "my dear sir," uttered with icy scorn in which there was no longer the slightest trace of irony, sent a shiver even down Otto's spine. Cousin drained his glass mechanically but made no sign of protest and said nothing in reply. Gleicher paused for a moment, then continued:

"Here are my orders, my dear sir. I'm sure that you appreciate the situation you're in and that I need not call your attention to the unpleasantness in store for you at the first sign of disobedience. . . . Oh, dear, I can tell from the look in your eyes that you don't understand. I'm not a complete savage. If our secret police, like the police of any other country, happens to number a few subordinates who debase themselves by the use of torture, I myself scorn these practices and never use them. You have nothing to fear from me on that score; I give you my word of honor as a German officer. No, if you don't toe the line, my dear sir, I shall merely see that your superiors in London get a copy of this tape recording."

PART FOUR

23   Austin entered Dr. Fog's office, as usual admiring the peace and quiet that reigned there. Engaged on more and more absorbing tasks of his own, Dr. Fog had left the Arvers case entirely in Austin's hands, with the proviso that he was to be notified of any important development. Deciding that at this juncture he needed his advice, Austin had applied for an interview. Dr. Fog greeted him with his usual affability.

"I've got some news for you, sir."

"Really?" Dr. Fog exclaimed, rubbing his hands together.

"First of all, this message that came in last week."

"From Arvers?"

"Yes. I thought you'd better have a look at it."

The doctor read it under his breath, pausing now and then for reflection.

"FRESH DEVELOPMENTS WITH GLEICHER. HAS BEEN CON-
TACTED BY SENIOR ABWEHR OFFICER WHO CLAIMS TO KNOW
ABOUT MY ACTIVITY AND HIS. PSEUDONYM OTTO. OTTO AS
WELL AS ABWEHR HEADQUARTERS CONVINCED GERMANY
HAS LOST WAR SEEKS CONTACT WITH ALLIED SECRET SERV-
ICE AUTHORITIES FOR EXTREMELY IMPORTANT NEGOTIA-
TIONS. CAUTION, BUT GLEICHER APPEARS TRUSTWORTHY.
WHAT ACTION SHOULD I TAKE?"

Dr. Fog showed no sign of surprise. Instead of giving
advice in reponse to Austin's tacit request, he simply
said:

"I suppose you've answered it already?"

"At once, sir, in the following terms: 'If you consider
offer genuine, establish contact with Otto yourself.
Obtain details and guarantees.'"

This message met with the doctor's approval.

"I felt this was the best course to follow, sir. Isolated as he is, there seems nothing against his meeting an enemy agent who in any case knows all about
him already. Furthermore . . . "

"Furthermore, when a trap has been set, we must
always pretend to fall into it. It's an excellent principle when dealing with mental cases and enemy secret
services. . . . But perhaps this isn't a trap."

"Perhaps it isn't, sir," Austin echoed without much
conviction.

"We mustn't automatically discourage an approach
of this kind, however strange it may seem. You realize,
of course, who the head of the *Abwehr* is?"

"Admiral Canaris."

"That's right. Now, this may surprise you, but there
have already been several rumors that he's trying to get
in touch with us. I mean, with someone of importance

in the service," Dr. Fog corrected himself with a hypocritical smile.

"Really?"

"Furthermore, some people are convinced that he's only waiting for a sign from us to come over to our side—which seems a little far-fetched, to say the least. . . . Did Arvers answer your message?"

"Yes, sir, like this: 'Have met Otto. Evidently important person and seems genuine. Guarantees: firstly, has shown he knows all about Gleicher's treachery, information provided, my own activities, links with London, radio wave lengths. Enough to have us all shot, yet has always left us undisturbed. Secondly, has himself provided me with documents I believe to be of great importance on which urgent action needed. Anxious establish contact with responsible authorities.' "

"What about these documents?" Dr. Fog asked.

"They arrived yesterday," Austin told him. "I passed them on to the specialists after glancing through them myself. All our opinions agree. They're infinitely more important than anything else we've had, and they appear to be accurate."

"How so?"

"We've been able to cross-check quite a number of them. There are some that refer to the new submarine shelter, on which a group of French engineers has already provided information; but these are far more complete and detailed. Others, covering a wider field, should prove extremely useful. Unless, of course . . ."

"Unless they're all part of a vast deception scheme."

"That's exactly what the specialists think, sir. But they add: 'In which case it's an extremely high-level scheme, drawn up by a service in close contact with the High Command . . .' At all events, this seems to prove that it's definitely an *Abwehr* authority who is interested in us."

"Which doesn't make it any more reassuring," Dr. Fog muttered.

"There's also another reason why we should be on our guard, sir."

The doctor looked at him intently. Austin had lowered his voice, like a lecturer preparing an effect.

"It's this, sir. These last two messages were encyphered in a code only Arvers knows, one reserved for top-secret messages. Their importance certainly justifies this precaution. Claire therefore sent them off without knowing what they were all about."

"You're quite sure it was Claire who sent them?"

"Absolutely certain. I asked the operator who usually receives her and there's no doubt about it. You know how they can recognize an operator's 'touch' when transmitting, even better than a signature. So it must have been Claire who sent them. Only . . ."

"Only what?"

"She inserted a warning sign, sir. Two letters inverted in a certain group. That doesn't present any decoding difficulty for our experts and, according to prearrangements, it means we must be on our guard."

Dr. Fog wrinkled his brow but made no comment. Austin waited a moment, then went on earnestly:

"It's still too early to form an opinion, sir, but it's certain our team isn't getting on very well together. The use of the special code can only mean that Arvers is suspicious of Claire. Her signal proves his feelings are reciprocated. Since my job is to keep an eye on this team, my presence over there is indispensable."

"It's rather dangerous," the doctor observed, without betraying any further sign of surprise.

"It would probably be even more so to let him take action on his own. As for taking no action at all, you yourself pointed out that we might be missing a golden opportunity."

"Claire sounded the alarm," the doctor observed pensively.

"She might have done that just because Arvers did not let her into the secret. Her obsession is quite capable of affecting her reason. I've been afraid of that all along."

Dr. Fog, who had had ample opportunity to judge the merits of his assistant and who valued him more highly than ever, agreed to his plan. As was his custom, he allowed him the greatest freedom of action. Austin would keep an eye on the team, study the German offer on the spot, have an interview with Gleicher, and even with the famous Otto, if he thought he could afford to take this risk. Eventually he would arrange a meeting at a higher level. The doctor brought an end to this conversation by advising a policy of caution.

"Don't forget, Austin," he said as he showed him out, "that the professionals in our organization would never have employed an agent who had once fallen into enemy hands."

24   Colonel Count von Gleicher was certainly no savage. He even prided himself, and with reason, on being highly civilized. He was as fond of philosophy and the arts as he was of war. During his week ends at the villa, after he had finished with Arvers and his professional obligations, he would often spend the evenings listening to records of classical music or immerse himself in the works of some great thinker, either ancient or modern. It was these very qualities that had singled him out for an important position in the *Abwehr*.

He was also a man of absolute rectitude and imbued with a sense of military honor. And so, as he listened for the first time to Arvers' confession, if his immediate action was mental nausea and his only remark, *"Schwein!"*, he did not for a moment think of making an exception in this case to the rule he had set himself in his dealings with enemy agents. This was made manifestly clear when his assistant, Otto, stressed the importance of the tape recording in a manner he did not care for at all.

"We know he's a coward, Herr Doktor. We'll have no difficulty in getting whatever we want out of him."

"We'll have no difficulty," Gleicher agreed, looking at him directly, "but remember what I've told you. We are not the Gestapo and I did not take on this job to soil my hands."

"I know your views on that subject, Herr Doktor, and I have nothing but respect for them. But physical pressure was not what I had in mind. Seeing what a coward he is, I think the mere threat . . ."

Gleicher interrupted him sternly.

"There's no question of that, either. I will not countenance the specter of torture—or physical pressure, as you put it—in this service. I should not be able to sleep at night if I ever debased myself by methods like that. No, Otto, *psychological* means are what we shall use," he added in a gentler tone, "and in this particular case, to which I've given a great deal of thought, I'm certain the weapon we possess is infinitely more efficacious than violence."

"Perhaps," said Otto without much conviction.

"Have you really any doubt about it? Do you mean to say you still can't see what his position is with regard to his superiors? Don't you realize he has accused the other fellow of treachery and passed himself off as a hero? Nothing else can account for his having been entrusted with another mission. That being so, don't you think this man will do absolutely anything for us to keep his secret?"

Otto looked at his chief with surprise, then with admiration. He would never have believed him capable of such ingenuity. For a moment, but no more than a moment, he had a vague suspicion that this plan might involve him in a procedure even more cruel than the methods of the Gestapo, but the evidence of its efficacy prevented these qualms from assuming definite shape and he merely replied:

"You're right, Colonel"—this was the first time he had addressed Gleicher by his military rank—"he is *obliged* to obey us. It's unpardonable of me not to have realized that before. I'm grateful to you for opening my eyes to the immorality and the uselessness of torture."

"*Ein Herrendienst,* Otto," Gleicher concluded, grinning with delight at this tribute.

Arvers did not offer the slightest resistance when Gleicher took him in hand. Such an effort was beyond him. The vague apprehension in which he had been living until then was succeeded by a palpable terror in the form of a ghastly vision that obtruded on him at every hour of the day and night.

The scene was Dr. Fog's office, which his memory depicted as the haunt of a mysterious and forbidding figure. The doctor was there with Austin and a number of French officers Arvers had known in London and who were full of admiration for his brilliant record. Claire had just come in, with that abominable smile on her lips. He himself was sitting in an armchair; the attention of the others was directed elsewhere.

Dr. Fog was examining with interest a flat, cylindrical object, turning it over in his nervous hands. At times his features reminded Arvers of Gleicher. He was saying:

"This has just arrived from France. This lady here brought it with her. An extremely interesting document, it seems."

"Extremely interesting, sir," Claire murmured.

"Extremely interesting, sir," Austin echoed.

"Very, very interesting indeed, sir," all his assistants repeated in unison, as though they knew what it was all about.

"We'll soon see," said Dr. Fog. "Someone bring me a tape recorder."

"A tape recorder, someone go and get a tape recorder! Where can we get hold of a tape recorder?" the rest of them chorused.

They scattered like a flock of sparrows and started hunting around the house, passing in and out of the room in frantic haste. The dream then assumed a particularly horrifying form for Arvers. During their interminably long search, he struggled feverishly but in vain to start his mind working. He cudgeled his brain passionately to find some means of preventing the audition. His mind, generally so fertile, was paralyzed by the weight of the problem and refused to work; his imagination was completely powerless; and his acute awareness of this total intellectual impotence was one of the most frightening aspects of his nightmare.

The machine was eventually brought in. Then all of a sudden, as though at the touch of a fairy's wand, the matrix imprisoning the workings of his brain seemed to dissolve and he recovered his mental powers. An idea came into his head by which he could avert the danger once and for all—an idea magnificent in its simplicity and which he greeted as a glorious miracle of his intelligence. But this glimmer of hope was instantly extinguished and his suffering assumed another form; for no sooner had he begun to congratulate himself on his marvelous discovery, no sooner had he been dazzled, in the incoherence of his hallucination, by the brilliance of this brain wave, than his physical paralysis, following on his mental impotence, hindered its execution. And so his ingenuity had shown itself in vain; for this amazing scheme consisted simply in his pouncing on the tape, tearing it into shreds, and swallowing the pieces!

Dr. Fog had picked up the cylinder again before he was able to lift a finger. He placed it on the machine with infinite care. Claire's laughter rang in his ears, a chant of triumph that intensified his torment. Arvers was now trying to channel his remaining energy into the muscles of his throat. His will was strained to the utmost in his effort to speak, to shout out loud, to drown the sound of the damnable machine that was already emitting his initial splutters, like the jarring voice of a demon announcing some infernal entertainment. But just when he thought he had succeeded, when the cry of salvation was about to issue from his lips, Dr. Fog noticed his presence. He now resembled Gleicher so closely that he might have been his twin. He silenced his victim with a lordly gesture.

All eyes were then turned on Arvers, and the lamentable note of entreaty in his voice resounded in the deathly hush: "I'll talk! I'll tell you everything, everything! I'll do anything you wish . . ."

25   The sound of that voice set in motion such painful vibrations in his body that he woke with a start. He was not in London but sprawled in an armchair in his living room, from which he had not moved for some time. He tried to persuade himself that this ridiculous dream was the product of a morbid imagination. It could not possibly happen like that in real life. He would find some way of warding off the danger. He had got himself out of many tight spots before. But first of all he would have to find a means of defense against this excruciating nightmare constantly hovering around him, waiting to overwhelm him the moment he was off guard. And in order to gain the upper hand in this struggle, his nature could conceive of only one weapon, one single stratagem—to charm away the diabolical obsession with the virtues of some other obsession of his own choosing and deliberately invoke a divine hallucination in colors bright enough to obliterate the first. He sometimes actually succeeded in doing so.

It was by no means an easy business. A desperate mental effort was needed for him to create the illusion that he was still a man of honor. Gleicher had done nothing to make this task any easier. He despised him to such an extent that he did not even bother to conceal his true intentions. He made no attempt to lend the least plausibility to the pretext he had invented in order to draw an important member of the Allied services into his clutches. His attitude could leave no doubt in Arvers' mind as to the infamy of his conduct. And yet, during those pathetic moments when he feverishly tried to find some antidote to the haunting nightmare, he frequently succeeded in convincing himself that his behavior had been dictated by an ardent sense of patriotism in the interests of the Allied cause. Such is the sovereign power of the human mind; such is its sublime dishonesty.

That day, as on every previous day, he racked his brains to conjure up the wretched arguments he considered fit to support this thesis, to furbish them with infinite patience and endow them with the quality needed to create his supreme illusion.

After all, though Gleicher did not attempt to persuade him of the purity of his intentions, the German had not actually said this was a case of deception. There was nothing to prove he was not genuinely seeking a means of collaboration. Admittedly, Arvers had been careful not to question him on this subject, for fear of receiving a forthright answer that would deprive him of all hope. This was a tenuous starting point, but enough for his dream to begin to take shape and eventually to illuminate the evidence of his integrity and perspicacity.

Then . . . then, in his mind's eye, he emerged as the promoter of one of the most important negotiations of the war. He, Arvers, the secret agent hunted by several police forces, whom his superiors did not provide with means worthy of him, accomplished the feat of leading the enemy to believe in their defeat and to surrender. Few characters in history had maneuvered with such Machiavellian cunning. Of all the masters of intrigue whose names he recalled, none had solved a problem comparable to this, or under such difficult conditions. And it was in his apparent submission to Gleicher that his ingenuity showed itself most strikingly. In fact, it was he who inspired every step the German took and directed every move he made, without his realizing it.

Usually he did not develop his romantic fancy beyond this stage: the submission of the *Abwehr*, brought about by his stratagems and by the influence he secretly exercised over Gleicher. He derived considerable comfort from the mere contemplation of this simple result and, in view of recent events, seemed to feel a sort of reluctance to venture toward more complicated ideas.

Today, however, he felt bold enough to let the hallucination grow in beauty and in power, follow its natural course unimpeded, gradually encroach upon those regions forbidden to the common run of humanity, and finally erupt into the glorious realm of his former chimeras, reviving the exaltation he had previously enjoyed:

The blow delivered against the enemy had to be exploited immediately. Arvers acted with the speed of lightning. Admiral Canaris having offered his services to the Allies, Arvers now demanded—he no longer dealt with any but the highest authority; Gleicher was restricted to a liaison role—he now demanded that Canaris arrest the Führer as proof of his loyalty. He would allow no evasion, no delay, no excuse. The plot organized under his auspices succeeded beyond the wildest hopes. Hitler and the entire High Command were captured. They were handed over to him one night, bound hand and foot, and he took them back with him to England after countless adventures. This was his last mission. The news of this capture suddenly burst upon the world, leading to an immediate cessation of hostilities. The rumor began to spread that this exploit was the feat of a single individual, an unknown hero who was only now allowed to come out into the open. It was not long before these rumors were confirmed by official announcements.

The sudden revelation of his valor marked the culminating point of his dream, the well-nigh inaccessible summit toward which all his efforts were directed and beyond which it was impossible to progress any further. Even to maintain a footing there made a considerable demand on his intellectual resources and, as usual, involved a number of precise material details to bolster his enthusiasm. He promptly applied himself to this task, exploring the various means of communication by which the news would, to use the expression he kept turning over in his mind, "burst upon the world"—the press, the radio . . . The idea of the radio was especially attractive. He paused for a moment at the vision of a typical family group gathered around their radio, listening to the startling announcement and repeating his name to one another with deference and admiration.

The telephone rang. A deathly chill gripped his body and mind, destroying the fruits of his heroic labor. At once he was plunged into the misery of reality all over again. A recently acquired reflex sent him rushing over to the instrument to lift the receiver before the initial ring had ceased. He knew what to expect. This was not the first time that Gleicher or Otto, eager to maintain their ascendency, reminded him of their presence in this way. He no longer dared to move from the living room for fear Claire might answer the phone.

It was Gleicher's voice, and in the background he could hear a faint buzzing sound.

"Listen, Herr Arvers!"

He was familiar with the ritual of these calls. The German would bring the tape recorder up to the mouthpiece. With the receiver glued to his ear, Arvers would then wait for the words he knew by heart, and which sounded more and more odious to him each time he heard them. As usual, the tape had been switched on before the call was put through, so that by now it had reached the essential passage: "I'll tell you everything, everything! I'll do whatever you wish . . ." The machine was then moved away from the telephone and Gleicher's commanding voice broke in:

"Can you hear me, Herr Arvers? Can you hear me all right? Why don't you answer?"

"I can hear you," Arvers replied in a muffled whisper.

"Your friends in London seem to be taking their time. . . . You can't do anything about it? I think you can, you know. You have their confidence; it's merely a question of persuading them to make up their minds. You ought to know better than I do how to convince them. Don't forget I'll hold you responsible if there's any hitch."

He fell silent for a moment. The buzzing sound could still be heard at the other end of the line. Arvers could no longer distinguish the words but contrived to grasp the meaning from the intonation, as Gleicher continued:

"Perhaps you think I haven't the means to carry out my threat? Don't deceive yourself, Herr Arvers. Only today I was thinking of the various possible methods. There are any number, but there's one in particular that appeals to me because of its simplicity, and also, I must admit, its originality. What do you think of this as an idea—include the recording in one of our routine broadcasts? How do you feel about that? I suppose you know that all your secret services make a point of listening in to Radio Paris—not to mention at least twenty million Frenchmen. . . . I hope I've made myself clear, Herr Arvers. I only wanted to be sure you weren't thinking of kicking against the pricks, as the saying goes."

He had finished speaking, but Arvers heard him bring the tape recorder back again so he would not miss the final words. At last there was a click at the other end of the line. He slumped weakly into the armchair. The nightmare was already hovering above his head, ready to bear down on him, and there was no longer any possibility of summoning his fantasies to the rescue. Gleicher's threat to broadcast the tape had the effect of an icy shower on him, shriveling once and for all the apotheosis of his dream and making a mockery of his deep spiritual struggles.

In this way Colonel Count von Gleicher occasionally reminded Arvers of his presence, at irregular intervals and at various times of day. He had the mind of a gentleman and not a policeman, as he never ceased to proclaim. His sense of honor bristled at the thought of resorting to physical pressure to break down a human being's resistance. The noble and infinitely more effective weapon he had decided to use in this special form of warfare (he had impressed this on Otto, who had at last understood) was *psychology*.

26   "I heard him. I remember the words exactly. He shouted: 'I'll tell you everything, I'll do whatever you wish.' And again, later on: 'I can be extremely useful to you; I have the confidence of my superiors.' What more do you want as proof of his treachery?"

Deeply moved by Claire's agitation, Austin gently increased the pressure of his arm around her shoulder to try to calm her down.

He had returned to France a few days earlier but had not yet notified Arvers of his arrival. He wanted to have a word with his companion first. He had sent her a message at her mother's, fixing a rendezvous in front of the movie house at Rennes, where they used to meet. They had exchanged no more than a word or two before taking their seats side by side in the darkness of the half-empty auditorium. Austin leaned toward her, put his arm around her shoulders, brought his face up close to hers, and started questioning her under his breath. He had already noticed what a nervous state she was in. She was clearly at the end of her tether, and her condition was a source of anxiety to him, both as a doctor and as head of the mission. At the same time he could not suppress a feeling of pity, intensified by the position he had adopted, which made him acutely aware of the trembling of her body.

Her opening words did nothing to reassure him as to her mental balance. She had meant to give him a methodical account of how her suspicions had developed and had then been confirmed during one of Gleicher's nocturnal visits, but she lost control of herself as soon as she mentioned Arvers' name. Her fury was manifested in sudden violent outbursts, and he had to caution her several times to lower her voice.

"My brother wasn't a traitor. It was Arvers, only Arvers, all the time."

All the symptoms of an obsession, Austin thought to himself with a sigh. For the last few months her only purpose in living has been to justify her brother by proving the other man's guilt, and now it's beginning to take the form of hallucinations. Has the first result of my boss's diabolical policy been to derange her mind?

He went on questioning her with infinite patience, concealing his skepticism.

"You say you heard him?"

"Utterly despicable, it sounded. One would have sworn he was groveling at the German's feet."

He asked her to try to put things in their proper order. She made a great effort to pull herself together and started on her story from the beginning.

Puzzled by the change in Gleicher's attitude that night, she had followed behind when he and Arvers went out of the house and had watched them go into the villa next door. There she had paused for some time. She was furious with herself for having hesitated so long, and her mother had since reproached her in the strongest terms. With a little more presence of mind, she could have heard the beginning of the conversation. She had eventually decided to slip into the garden and had crept up to one of the windows. With her ear glued to the shutters, she had heard the sound of a man's voice and could distinguish a word here and there. It was Arvers' voice, she was absolutely certain. He seemed to be gasping for breath and in the grip of a mortal terror. She had remembered one phrase of his, word for word: "I'll tell you everything, everything! I'll do whatever you wish"; then, a little later on: "I can be extremely useful to you; I have the confidence of my superiors." As though begging for mercy. At first she thought they were torturing him, but she had examined him closely and he showed no signs of ill-treatment on his return. No doubt Gleicher had merely threatened him, and that had been all that was needed.

After that? Someone drew the heavy curtains behind the window, muffling the sounds from within, and she had not been able to hear any more. But wasn't that enough? That was what must have happened at the Lachaume farm. He was the one who had talked, not her brother.

Austin peered at her in the darkness, unable to come to any conclusion, trying desperately to find something in her expression on which to base a diagnosis. It was quite possible she had imagined the whole thing as a result of misinterpreting an odd phrase here and there. Yet he was impressed by the continuity of her account and by her faithful repetition of the words Arvers had used. She had now mastered her emotions sufficiently to give him further details.

"Ever since then he has been a different man. He is even more suspicious of me than before. He has had a few more meetings with Gleicher, but he's the one who always puts himself out and goes over to the villa next door. He has received a number of telephone calls, during which he himself hardly says a word, apart from replying in a terrified voice: 'Yes . . . Certainly . . . I understand . . .' After each call he looks completely washed out. He lies sprawled in his chair, on the point of collapse. He never moves out of arm's reach of the telephone—he's afraid I might answer it . . . But I'm going to find out what they say to him. I've now got the means at my disposal."

"What means?"

She told him without a moment's hesitation that the day before, while Arvers was out of the house visiting Gleicher, she had taken the opportunity to connect one of her receivers to the telephone line. From her room she could now listen in to all their conversations.

Austin disapproved of this procedure but, bearing in mind the importance of a possible betrayal, he felt he had no right to question it. Furthermore, she was so completely convinced of Arvers' villainy that no amount of reasoning would have changed her opinion. The best thing was to let her go ahead, take advantage of her scheme, which results would justify if she was right and which would expose her mistake if she was wrong—unless, of course, she was completely out of her mind? He looked at her again. She seemed to read his thoughts and forced herself to speak more calmly.

"Don't think I'm letting my imagination run away with me. I swear there was no mistake about it. I jotted down his words that very evening so as to make quite sure. You can have a look at my notebook if you like."

The recovery of her composure strongly influenced Austin's decision. In a few minutes he drew up his plan of battle. First he told her briefly the contents of the top-secret messages and the outlines of Gleicher's proposal. She distrusted the whole business and would look upon it only as a trap set with Arvers' complicity. Austin discussed it no further and gave her her instructions.

"I'll phone him tomorrow to let him know I've arrived. I'll tell him that the Allies are interested in the offer and I have come to look into it more closely, which is actually true. I'll ask him to arrange for me to meet Gleicher and Otto. He'll have to phone them. And then . . ."

He had a final twinge of conscience, which was swiftly dispelled by the recollection of Dr. Fog's last words of advice.

"And then you will listen carefully to every word they say and take it all down. After that we'll be able to see whether I ought to keep the appointment and what precautions I'll have to take. Whatever you do, be careful not to rouse their suspicions."

194

She promised to do exactly as he said. They left the auditorium without being noticed and parted outside the movie. He stood there for some time, puzzled, watching her as she moved away and was finally swallowed up in the crowd.

27   "Is that you, Herr Arvers? What, you're surprised I recognize your voice? But it's very characteristic, you know; no one who has heard it once is likely to forget it. What can I do for you . . . ? Yes, yes, I see, very interesting. At last! Hold the line a moment, will you . . ."

Gleicher frequently assumed this bantering tone with Arvers. He seemed to delight in alternately terrifying and humiliating him. He put his hand over the mouthpiece to say softly to Otto, who was sitting opposite him writing:

"They're biting."

Otto interrupted his work and took the receiver his chief handed to him.

"Really? Someone very important, you say?"

"It's my immediate superior from London," Arvers

replied. "He has already been here. He is familiar with all the French side of the business and has been detailed to arrange a meeting with someone of even greater importance."

This was exactly what Austin had told him to say. Claire, who was listening in upstairs, heaved a sigh of disappointment at hearing not a single suspect word. True, Gleicher's tone was slightly peculiar, but that was not sufficient proof for Austin.

"Where will the meeting be held? But at your place, of course, Herr Arvers. You know what confidence I have in you! Naturally there'll just be the two of you, no one else."

"Naturally," Arvers replied.

Gleicher fixed the meeting for the evening two days ahead, then continued in a tone of authority:

"I don't think I need remind you again to stick to my instructions."

Claire's hopes soared. She underlined the word "instructions" in the notebook in which she was taking down the conversation.

"I hope you haven't said anything that could rouse your chief's suspicions?"

"I've adhered to our agreement to the letter."

"Our *agreement!*"

Arvers' use of this term was a halfhearted endeavor not to lose face in his own eyes. He could not regard himself as a traitor: he was merely acting as an intermediary in some tricky negotiations between enemy leaders, that was all. Away from Gleicher, he had plucked up enough courage to use this word, which cast a reassuring light on the transaction.

"Our *agreement!*"

The sarcasm contained in the exclamation cut him to the quick. In the margin of her notebook, Claire recorded these changes in tone by a system of conventional signs. For all his anger, Arvers did not dare answer back. Once again he was frightened of receiving a reply that would shatter all his illusions.

He ventured, however, to ask for further details on one particular point. He did so with a note of entreaty in his voice, after having sworn to himself several times in the past twenty-four hours that he would take a firm line when discussing the deal.

"You did say, didn't you, Mr. Gleicher, that if all goes well . . . that if you're satisfied with my services," he added in a wheedling tone, "you would give me the roll?"

This—the only demand he had made from the very beginning—was almost in the nature of a condition he had steeled himself to impose. Gleicher had agreed to it, to save himself a fruitless argument.

Claire scribbled this down, then paused in bewilderment, waiting for a further explanation.

"The roll? What roll?"

The questions and answers succeeded one another at sufficiently long intervals for her to have time to grasp the general meaning and also appreciate the various fine distinctions. The more humble Arvers' tone became, the more impatient and sarcastic was Gleicher's. As a matter of fact, the word "agreement" had filled him with cold fury and he was only pretending not to understand so as to force Arvers to confess his ignominy out loud, well aware what such a confession would cost him even in the absence of witnesses. The same sort of urge had led him to make not the slightest effort to conceal his maliciousness. He refused to allow Arvers the meager satisfaction that even the mildest reassurance on that score would have brought him.

"What roll do you mean?" he repeated, after a heavy silence on Arvers' part.

"But . . . surely you know . . ."

"Surely I know what? I haven't the faintest idea what you're talking about, I assure you."

He was deliberately taunting. Arvers clenched his fists, fully aware of the man's insidiousness. Rage made his voice sound less obsequious as he replied:

"I'm referring to the record, the ribbon—I don't know the exact term for it."

"Oh, you mean"—the tone of polite remonstrance was more insulting than the worst abuse—"you mean the tape? You must talk properly, Herr Arvers. Now I understand. You mean the tape that brings back such unpleasant memories of the Lachaume farm?"

Claire gave a start. Her emotion was so intense that she almost dropped her pen. Arvers continued, in his previous wheedling tone:

"You promised you would let me have it."

"That fascinating document in which you more than gratify the wishes of those Gestapo swine? One might almost say you even went beyond their demands, Herr Arvers. That's the one you mean, isn't it? You know, I never get tired of listening to that tape and I think I have detected some extremely interesting details that had escaped me before and that perhaps you may not have noticed yourself. Yes, toward the end there's a sort of moaning sound in the background that could not have come from you. I just wondered whether it might be the voice of your colleague—that colleague of yours who, unlike you, gave only a few inarticulate screams. That's the tape you mean, isn't it?"

Claire forced herself to write this down without giving further thought to it. If she had allowed herself a moment's pause to think about the meaning of these words, she would have been incapable of continuing.

"That's the one," Arvers said in an almost inaudible voice. "You promised . . ."

Gleicher interrupted him in biting tones:

"Well then, if I promised, that ought to satisfy you, I should think."

He had noticed a strange gleam in the eyes of his assistant, Otto. He suddenly felt ashamed of his own behavior and wanted to put an end to this conversation as quickly as possible.

"A German officer never breaks his word. I'll keep my promise if you toe the line. You can be quite sure I won't forget to bring this document with me to the rendezvous, Herr Arvers. So if anything should happen to me, your chief would find it on me. . . . See you the day after tomorrow."

"Thank you," Arvers replied in a strangled voice.

Gleicher subsided into a moody silence, well aware that Otto was gazing at him with curiosity.

"*Schwein!*" he finally muttered.

The abuse was obviously intended for Arvers, but he did not feel especially pleased with himself, either. He was shocked to realize that he sometimes took a sly pleasure in tormenting his victim, although his task did not always justify such an attitude. He began to wonder if his new profession wasn't developing a certain sadistic trait in his character.

He shrugged his shoulders, trying to think of some other subject to dispel his feeling of uneasiness. Of course he would let him have the tape, since this was what he had promised. But how could that abject creature also be so stupid? Weren't they taught in the enemy schools that nothing was easier to copy than a document of that sort? A mere child would have suspected that there were already several copies safely filed away. This led him to consider his own duplicity again; then he pulled himself together and dismissed these unwelcome thoughts from his mind.

"You heard, didn't you, Otto? It's for the day after tomorrow, in the evening. We've barely got time to make all the necessary arrangements."

"Don't you think, Herr Doktor, that your security demands a few extra precautions?"

"Not at all. We shall go there by ourselves. We must inspire this envoy from London with confidence, which should be easy if we play our cards properly. This is a matter of brains, not brawn—a question of psychology, as I've told you before, Otto. We've nothing to fear from this fellow, Arvers. He's much too cowardly to do us any harm, and we have him too firmly in our clutches."

"I was thinking more of his chief. I find it hard to believe he doesn't suspect anything."

"He does suspect something, I'm sure, but our plans have been well thought out and organized through various other channels as well. The story should sound plausible. What it boils down to is a battle of wits. And besides, don't imagine that the man we're going to meet the day after tomorrow is the head of the Intelligence Service. After all, they're not complete beginners, and will have sent a mere envoy. But I'm aiming much higher than that. That's why we have to gain this man's confidence, and we have enough original documents to show him to achieve this. It's big game we're after, Otto."

Gleicher always saw far ahead and had a knack of appearing to see even farther. His contempt for the Gestapo, which aimed only at easy and immediate results, prompted him to take a completely different line. Moreover, after a confidential meeting with the head officer of the *Abwehr,* he had succeeded in arranging for a considerable effort to be made by various other branches so that his offer to open negotiations might appear quite genuine. He held a number of trumps in his hand and had made up his mind to bring off a master stroke. There was a hint of condescension in his voice as he gave Otto his final instructions.

"Be sure you get completely into the character you're playing, Otto. You're the Number One, remember, a senior *Abwehr* officer who has the ear of the Admiral. I shall remain in the background; I'm merely an intermediary who's out for what he can get. As far as Arvers is concerned, it doesn't matter at all; but in the presence of his chief we've got to stick to our respective roles. Any change would make him suspicious."

Otto assured him that he had long since had ample opportunity to study the behavior of senior German officers and *Abwehr* officials. He felt sure he could put on a flawless performance. He gave a brief demonstration of his skill then and there; whereupon Colonel Count von Gleicher first wrinkled his brow, then, on second thought, gave a faint smile and deigned to declare himself satisfied.

28   Austin arrived at Mrs. Morvan's grocery just as it was getting dark. Claire was waiting for him there. He had not gotten in touch with her earlier for fear of rousing Arvers' suspicions. Since the meeting with the Germans was to take place that evening, Arvers had asked Claire to spend the night at her mother's place so as to leave the villa free for him, as he had some confidential business to attend to there.

She showed Austin into the back parlor, where the old woman came and joined them after closing the shutters, and gave him a faithful account of the telephone conversation.

"It's all quite clear to me now," she concluded. "What I overheard in the garden was part of the tape recording referring to the Lachaume farm affair. It's conclusive proof of his treachery and of my brother's innocence. The Germans have him in their clutches and are using him to lead you into a trap."

Austin was overwhelmed by this precise report and by the details in her notebook. It was a strange story, but probably true. It was difficult to attribute this long and graphic conversation to an hallucination. He questioned her closely again, then turned toward her mother, who had not yet said a word. He knew she had a domineering personality. With him, she generally assumed an air of indifference, as though all this business meant nothing to her. This evening, however, he detected a trace of anxiety in her expression; she seemed to be studying his reactions. And he needed only this fleeting glint in her eyes to remind him that she was Morvan's mother; her usual attitude tended to make him forget it.

He began to wonder if the two women, far from being slightly unbalanced, had not deliberately invented the whole story to redeem the memory of the deceased, no matter what the consequences. Such a disregard for justice in the cause of a deep devotion made him shudder, but considering the old woman's obdurate expression and Claire's blazing eyes, this monstrous supposition did not seem entirely impossible. He eventually dismissed it from his mind, reproaching himself for seeing nothing but treachery and lies ever since he had become Dr. Fog's assistant.

"This meeting is a trap," Claire insisted. "What Gleicher said proves that he still regards us as mortal enemies."

Austin read through her notes again, paused for a moment to think, then said with authority:

"I'd like to watch them without their knowing

it. I've got to see for myself what sort of attitude they adopt. Can that be arranged?"

"We could get right up to the villa if we approached it through the wood . . . and even slip into the garden without anybody noticing. There's an old ruined tower in one corner, from which you can keep a lookout in all directions. It's a perfect hiding place."

It was clear she had already used this observation post. He wasted no time on further questions and fell in with her plan. They decided to leave at once so as to arrive well before the meeting and thus avoid any possible trap. Without a trace of emotion, the old woman wished them good luck and watched them in silence as they vanished into the dark. It was not until she had carefully locked up for the night that she mumbled a few indistinct words in a menacing tone, almost without unclenching her teeth.

Austin followed Claire quietly. He had decided to rely on her entirely until he could form his own opinion. As soon as they were outside the village she led the way across some open fields, then through a rather heavily wooded area where the cold made him shiver. He shook off the anxieties that were preying on his mind to devote himself to the more urgent business of trying to avoid revealing their presence. She walked straight ahead without hesitation, although it was pitch dark. On two occasions, when he put his hand on her shoulder so as not lose touch with her, he noticed she was feverishly hot.

She slackened her pace, came to a halt behind a thicket, and whispered in his ear:

"This is the place."

They were almost at the front gate, which had been left half open. After listening for a moment or two, Claire gave a sign for him to follow her. They crossed a path, slipped into the garden, crept along the fence, and entered a sort of tower that must have served at one time as a pigeon loft. This was her hiding place. It had a ladder that gave access to the roof. They climbed up and made themselves as comfortable as possible so as to be able to wait for a long time without shifting their positions.

A crescent moon was beginning to shed its light over the wood. At the end of the garden, the white front of the villa stood out clearly against the trees. Thanks to a passing cloud, Austin was able to make out a faint glimmer behind the shutters of the living room. He tried to visualize Arvers waiting there for his visitors.

The wood all around them appeared to be deserted. After peering into the dark patch of each thicket, he could see nothing to rouse his suspicions. Claire pointed out Gleicher's villa, some fifty yards farther on. In that direction, too, everything seemed quite peaceful. They had arrived well ahead of time. They waited like this for almost two hours, on the alert for the slightest sound, but without detecting anything to justify their caution.

Suddenly she touched his shoulder, but he, too, had seen it—a rectangle of light in front of Gleicher's villa. Two silhouettes were visible for an instant; then the door closed behind them without a sound.

"Only two of them, as agreed," Austin whispered.

She made no reply. After a minute or two the figures reappeared on the path and passed immediately below them. Claire pointed out Gleicher: she had recognized him by his limp, although his face was partly hidden in a scarf. He had always been sensitive to cold and dreaded the damp at night.

They stopped in front of the gate, scrutinized the house and the immediate surroundings for some time, then entered the garden. Austin, who was observant by nature and whose every sense was quickened, noticed that Gleicher's companion stood aside to let him pass through. He also observed that Gleicher made a gesture of impatience and muttered something under his breath, whereupon Otto hurried in ahead of him. This little scene, on the face of it insignificant, started off a train of thought in Austin's mind; but for the moment he did not follow it to its logical conclusion, so eager was he not to miss a single detail of the next act.

Arvers must have been on the lookout, for he opened the front door before the Germans even had time to knock, and came out to meet them. For a moment he stood in full light, and Austin was struck by the change in his appearance.

"He hasn't arrived yet."

"Yet we've taken the trouble to be here on time," said Otto, who was now playing his part with authority.

"I don't think he'll be much longer," Arvers replied timidly.

The three men went inside and the door closed behind them, much to the disappointment of Austin, who was anxious to hear more. In the darkness and ensuing silence, Claire and he then started to keep a close watch on Gleicher's villa, since they felt that any danger was bound to come from that direction. But the house was now fully visible in the light of the moon and appeared to be fast asleep.

They went on waiting for another half hour. At least twenty times Austin was tempted to climb down from his observation post and keep the appointment. Finally he glanced at his companion, who seemed dreadfully disappointed, and said almost regretfully:

"It doesn't look like a trap to me. There are only two of them. I'm going down to join them. Wait for me here."

He was just getting up to leave when an impression recorded a short time before suddenly flashed through his mind—the behavior of the two Germans at the front gate: Otto's instinctive move to step aside, and Gleicher's gesture of protest, which looked like a reprimand. He followed the train of thought that had been started off at the time and came to the only logical conclusion: Gleicher was the real chief. He was the one behind the whole scheme; he had organized it down to the last detail. Why this deception, then, unless with a hostile aim in view? The time it took him to work out this problem in his mind prevented him from putting his plan into action. He was still hesitating when there was a sound of footsteps inside the house. Presently the three men emerged under the light at the entrance.

This abortive meeting had infuriated Gleicher. In his anger he forgot to confine himself to his role of subordinate and assumed his usual arrogant manner.

"My dear sir," he said in an icy tone, "do you really think I'm going to wait here all night for your chief to turn up? He should have been here an hour ago."

"I can't understand it," Arvers stammered. "He must

have been unavoidably detained. I did all I possibly could, I assure you."

"I'm only interested in results. I warned you I'd hold you responsible if anything went wrong."

A note of entreaty crept into Arvers' voice.

"Just give me one more chance. I assure you I really did persuade him to agree to this meeting. I'm sure to hear from him sooner or later, and I'll arrange another appointment at once."

Gleicher hesitated, but the business was too important for him to refuse.

"All right then," he finally agreed, "one last chance —the last chance for *you*. I hope I've made myself clear, Herr Arvers?"

"He may still turn up tonight, for all I know."

"We're not prepared to wait indefinitely. Besides, Otto has to get back to Paris. No, it's off for tonight . . . Just the same," he added after a moment's reflection, "if you do hear from him, let me know. Is that clear? It's your last chance, remember, Herr Arvers."

29   Austin could hear only part of this conversation, but it was enough to lend weight to Claire's accusation: Arvers really seemed to be a tool in the Germans' hands. He was about to go and ask him to account for himself when she suddenly motioned to him to sit down. A faint sound had attracted her attention. The front door opened again and a figure furtively approached the threshold. All the lights inside the house had been switched off, but the sky was sufficiently clear for them to recognize the figure as Arvers. He paused on the doorstep, half hidden behind a pillar, and remained there, motionless and silent, peering out into the darkness.

Alone in the villa after the Germans had left, Arvers had lapsed into a state of gloom.

Austin had not turned up. The reason was obvious:

he was suspicious—suspicious of the Germans, of course, but also of him, Arvers. His unique sensitivity to what other people thought about him was infallible. From the tone of Austin's voice over the telephone, he had been able to tell that the Englishman's suspicions were aroused by something in his own behavior.

In spite of his dismay, he made an effort to reason with himself dispassionately. What would he himself, the craftiest agent of all, have done if he had suspected a trap? He would have pretended to agree to the meeting and then discreetly kept the place under close observation without revealing his presence. That was probably how Austin had acted. Perhaps he was still lying in wait at this very moment?

It was at this stage of Arvers' deductions that he left the house, after turning out all the lights. The darkness and the silence excited him; his nerves were already strained beyond endurance by the ordeals of the last few months. Suddenly the forest seemed extraordinarily hostile, concealing in the shadow of every bush someone bent on his destruction. His enemies—by whom he meant anyone who discussed him behind his back—he imagined those enemies gathered together this evening in this secluded corner of Brittany, temporarily united in their common feeling of ill-will toward him. Dr. Fog, who had entrusted him with this mission only in order to bring about his ruin, was undoubtedly one of them. Claire was also there, in the forefront. She must have told them about him and guided them to his hide-out. Austin had talked it over with her before telephoning him—probably at her mother's, that old witch who hated him even more than did the others.

What could she have said about him? She loathed

and despised him in spite of the heroism of which he had given ample proof. To have risked his life twenty times over, courted danger every minute of the day, contended with a menacing brute regardless of the consequences—all this was to no avail. He had been prepared to liquidate Bergen. He had changed his mind only from a sense of duty, to avoid the inevitable reprisals and the death of dozens of innocent people. And that idiot girl had jumped to the conclusion that he was frightened of meeting a man face to face and killing him! The absurdity of this idea brought a smile to his lips. How little she knew him! He had proved himself in this respect as well, but he could scarcely flaunt his prowess in broad daylight.

He shook his head to prevent the revival of other memories that threatened to set his thoughts on a sinister course. It was his immediate enemies that mattered tonight, particularly Claire. It was Claire's opinion that he had to contend with. To her he would always be a coward; nothing would make her change her mind. Nothing, except perhaps . . .

He turned back into the house for a moment and disappeared from view. He had no definite purpose in mind—it was simply that he thought he had seen a glimmer of hope in the darkness, and his subconscious had propelled him inside. He was away less than a minute. When he reappeared he was holding in his outstretched hands a small object that neither Claire nor Austin could distinguish clearly. Almost immediately he stuffed it into his pocket, keeping his fist clenched tightly around it.

A sudden beam of light illuminated the path as a car drove out of the garden of the villa beyond. Austin remembered what Gleicher had said: this was Otto leaving for Paris. The car soon vanished into the distance. From their observation post they could see Gleicher as he closed the gate before going inside. When Austin returned back in Arvers' direction, he could not see him anywhere until presently he emerged from the shadows where he had been crouching to avoid the headlights. At that instant he was clearly visible in the moonlight, and his gaze seemed to be fixed on one specific spot. His haggard face was turned in the direction of the other villa.

What had Claire reported? How much did she know, exactly? In spite of all his precautions, had he given himself away at any time during the months they had been living together, especially during the last few weeks? He could not be perpetually on guard; perhaps he might have said something in his sleep? Had she followed him to Gleicher's without his knowing it? She was capable of anything. And if she had, she might have . . .

He uttered an obscene oath. That must be it—she had heard the recording. It made such a noise, such an infernal din; even on the telephone it made his ears ring. . . . And she had faithfully sent every word of it back to London, by means of a special code. All his enemies, both in England and in France, were now aware of the existence of the tape. To get hold of it was the sole purpose of their maneuvers, for Claire's tittle-tattle was not enough; they had to have the material evidence in their hands. That was why Austin had come back to France, and his absence this evening assumed a deeper significance. Since Dr. Fog had ordered him to get hold of the tape at any price, naturally he had to get in touch with Gleicher, but without Arvers' being there.

The whole situation was gradually becoming clearer with each fresh pulsation of his fevered brain. Why should they need him, after all? They were simply waiting until he had gone to bed before going off to find Gleicher and make a deal with him. Gleicher would hand over the tape as proof of his good will, only too pleased with this opportunity to do him a bad turn. It was even more than likely that the whole thing had been arranged in advance. Gleicher had been leading him on the whole time. He had been mad to trust him—how can one ever trust a German? Gleicher obviously found it more profitable to negotiate with Austin than with him. Not only did they all look upon him as a coward but they considered him to be of no account.

There was no longer any doubt in his mind. Gleicher had stayed behind alone in the villa to negotiate the deal—alone with the tape recording.

This mixture of shrewdness and wild aberration culminated in a conclusion of such logic and purity that he experienced a kind of pleasure he had not known for a long time—the certainty of having recovered the strength and all the keenness of his intellect.

His fate depended on this document and on its present owner. Right now, in a single movement his subconscious had already planned and that his mind was now beginning to analyze in detail, he could not only get hold of it but could also confound his enemies by proving he was capable of accomplishing the most dreadful and most laudable feat of all. Theoretically, the plan was perfect. All that remained was to spur his body into action.

Well, he'd show them! The simplicity and beauty of his reasoning had kindled a fire in his flesh and muscles. To redeem his honor and at the same time compel his foes to recognize his true heroic stature just when they thought that victory was theirs— this was a prospect of intoxicating bliss, the only one acceptable to his supreme egotism, the only one that could overcome the instincts of his timid nature.

Before he could make up his mind to take the first step, the thought that had previously brought a haughty, contemptuous smile to his lips occurred to him again: Claire was absolutely devoid of perspicacity; he knew perfectly well he was capable of killing—in certain circumstances! He no longer tried to dismiss the horror from his mind. On the contrary, he derived an additional stimulation from contemplating it and, with his hand still clenched in his pocket, he strode out of the house.

30   "What on earth is he up to now?" Claire muttered in a voice that betrayed her nervous tension.

Arvers was creeping along the path toward Gleicher's villa as silently as a ghost. He paused for a moment at the front gate, then slipped into the garden. Austin had a feeling that the final act was yet to be played and motioned to his companion. They climbed down from the pigeon loft and in their turn crept up toward the villa, keeping in the shadow of the trees. Hiding behind some bushes, they heard a muffled sound of music: Gleicher was indulging in his favorite diversion. Cautiously parting the branches, they caught sight of Arvers twenty yards away in front of the door and on the point of knocking. He had been standing there all the time they were approaching.

The phonograph record must have drowned the sound, for there was no answer. Arvers waited a minute, then knocked again, more loudly and repeatedly. The music continued, but Austin presently heard Gleicher's voice.

"Who's that?"

"It's me," said Arvers. "I thought you wouldn't have gone to bed yet. I just wanted to let you know that my chief from London has turned up."

The door was held ajar, then flung wide open. The light from the hall blazed out into the garden. Gleicher glanced out and gave a scornful titter as he saw Arvers standing there alone.

"You almost frightened me, Herr Arvers. I wasn't expecting you, and all by yourself, too."

Austin saw Arvers wince at the insult, but his only reply was to apologize for the misunderstanding.

"It's not my fault," he said. "His car broke down and he had to borrow a bicycle. He's sorry he's so late, but he would very much like to meet you now if you would be kind enough to step over to my place."

"Otto has just left," Gleicher grumbled. "Nevertheless, there's no harm in having a preliminary talk. I'd like to know what he's like. . . . But does he think I'm at his beck and call? I've already inconvenienced myself once tonight."

Arvers assumed a still more obsequious tone.

"I don't quite know what to say. I think he's a bit suspicious, in spite of all I've told him. That's only natural; he doesn't know you. Besides, he thinks you're only an intermediary. I've told him you're prepared to be of service to him. Those were your own instructions."

Gleicher peered at him intently. He hesitated for some time, remembering the conversation he had had with Otto just before the latter left for Paris. Otto had said he didn't like the idea of leaving him there all alone, next door to a man who had every reason to hate him.

"Nonsense, Otto, I have nothing to fear from him. He hasn't the guts to do me any harm. When the Gestapo arrested him, he didn't lift a finger to resist them."

"Sudden violence paralyzes him," Otto had replied. "It may not be the same when he's given time to think."

This remark was sufficiently shrewd to have made Gleicher pause to consider it for a moment. He realized that his assistant was making some progress in the particular field to which he himself attached so much importance, namely psychology. But he could not accept the views of a subordinate on this subject.

"Not on your life," he retorted scornfully. "He's one of those people who are physically incapable of shedding blood, even to save their own lives."

"Yes, I agree, Herr Doktor, but there could be an even more powerful motive. . . . And talking about that Gestapo business, there's one point I still don't understand."

It seemed so very strange of Otto to pursue this argument, at the risk of incurring his chief's displeasure, that Gleicher asked him to explain himself.

"It's a detail that has always puzzled me and I've been thinking about it a great deal these last few days. How did his operator, Morvan, die? We've always assumed the Gestapo killed him. Well, now, I got in touch again with my agent, who interrogated the survivors all over again, and they still seem quite convinced about it."

"About what?"

"They swear that Morvan was already dead when they got back to the farm."

"As a result of the torture?"

"Not at all, Herr Doktor—as a result of several bullets in his heart."

Otto had made no further comment. Gleicher had given some thought to the matter, then shrugged his shoulders and dismissed his assistant, having made up his mind not to alter his plan.

The memory of that conversation made him feel slightly uneasy, but his pride would not allow him to heed the implicit warning.

"Very well, then," he said. "Since your chief's frightened, I'll come over to your place."

He glanced at the forest and shivered.

"Hang on a moment. I'm just going to get a coat."

He shut the door in Arvers' face and went back into the living room. Colonel von Gleicher's rheumatism did not take kindly to nocturnal walks in the country. He had lit a big log fire, in front of which he had planned to spend the rest of the evening listening to his favorite records, and he sighed at the prospect of leaving this warmth. He bundled himself up and reluctantly dragged himself away from the hearth. Before leaving the room he paused, retraced his steps, and, with a gesture of irritation, slipped a revolver into his pocket.

No sooner had Gleicher disappeared inside than Arvers grasped the handle of the door. He opened it without making a sound and slipped into the house close on the German's heels.

His physical appearance had undergone a change, as

always happened when he did violence to his nature. The blood had drained away from his face. His movements were those of an automaton controlled by an alien will that seemed out of proportion to his own and to which he surrendered himself with a sense of pleasant abandon. In spite of his fear, he was delighted to see that his muscles obeyed the imperative commands of his mind and that he was behaving like a man of exceptional courage. He knew that nothing would stop him now, and already regarded the act he was about to perform as over and done with.

This was not the first time he had let himself be guided by a sovereign power that overcame all his inner resistance. He concentrated on the vision that had obtruded on his mind's eye a moment before and that revealed itself as a source of inexhaustible energy. He savored it in every detail and once again exultantly relived the scene of that heroic precedent.

31   When the Gestapo men had brought him back to the room where Morvan was lying and left him under the guard of two of their colleagues, Cousin had spent what were undoubtedly the worst hours of his life. He had said as much to Dr. Fog and, like many of his statements, this one was perfectly true.

Sprawled in an armchair, he forced himself to keep absolutely still and to make his mind a complete blank. He made a desperate effort to divorce himself from reality by assuming the immobility and rigidity of a corpse. The only hope he allowed himself to cherish was an indefinite prolongation of this semiconscious state into which he had managed to submerge himself, thanks to the respite his executioners had granted him. He was afraid of the most commonplace manifestation of external activity that threatened to snatch him from this blessed and relatively painless inertia. The sound of a cock-crow in the middle of the night caused him an almost unbearable twinge.

He shut his eyes so as not to see Morvan, who was stretched out on the bed. The Gestapo men had bandaged him up casually, after treating his wounds with oil and actually uttering a few words of sympathy. Their task accomplished, there was no reason for them not to show a certain amount of pity. Reckoning there was nothing more to fear from him, they unloosened his fetters. Then, after testing Cousin's handcuffs and turning the key in the door, they sat down to a game of cards and opened the brandy they had come across while searching the house.

During the spells of anguish, when he could not prevent himself from thinking, Cousin presumed they would send a car in the morning and take him and Morvan off to prison. He dreaded the idea, not for fear of solitary confinement—on the contrary, he hoped he would have a cell to himself—but because of the ordeal to which he would be subjected in resuming contact with the material world.

A reflex, however, compelled him to open his eyes from time to time. Morvan had stopped groaning; he, too, lay quite still, his eyes shut tight. Yet they had been wide open when Cousin had come in and, though glazed with pain, had stared at him fixedly. Cousin had even succeeded, by means of a heroic effort, in dropping his servile manner; he straightened his back and held his head high. But a terrifying thought flashed through his mind at the very moment he adopted this pose—Morvan knew. The doors of both rooms had been left open and he himself had heard every scream. Morvan, therefore, was fully aware of his treachery; he had not lost consciousness in spite of his suffering. This was clear from the glint in his eyes; Cousin merely had to glance at them to recognize their piercing look of contempt, that manifestation of hostility that he dreaded more than anything. He detected yet another sentiment, equally odious to him—pride triumphant. The combination of these two expressions caused him intense pain, which became almost unbearable when Morvan added to it by smiling faintly—the same hateful token of derision he was to see later on Claire's lips.

Now at last Morvan had closed his eyes on his triumph and his contempt. They waited together like this for several hours, apparently forgotten by an enemy who had better things to attend to than them. Grateful for this unexpected period of leisure, their guards felt there was no immediate danger and gradually relaxed their vigilance.

Cousin struggled to maintain the same position of rigidity, hoping against hope that this respite would last forever. Suddenly, in one of those irresistible reflexes that compelled him to look at Morvan, he noticed a slight change in his posture: he had rolled over onto his side and was facing the Germans. The latter had finished their game and were now slumped in their chairs half asleep. Cousin noticed that his companion's gaze was fixed on the submachine gun that one of them had placed beside him. With slow, almost imperceptible movements, he drew back his blanket, while his eyes judged the distance between him and the weapon.

He was clearly preparing to perform some desperate act. He tested the strength of his arms to see if they could supplement the thrust of his crippled legs. Cousin hated him even more for making this attempt: he regarded as sacrilege anything that threatened to drag him out of his voluntary torpor. He was filled with rage at the idea of being snatched out of the only state he found bearable, and especially by Morvan, who only wanted to humiliate him further by a gesture of absurd temerity.

If he did not cry out to warn the guards, it was only because he was once again completely paralyzed. The prospect of violence had deprived him of the power of speech. Dumfounded and petrified, he could only look on as Morvan made his final preparations. He did not move a muscle when the latter threw back his blanket and, shoving himself forward with his arms, snatched up the submachine gun and mowed down the guards with a couple of bursts before collapsing himself, overcome with pain.

The sound of the firing was succeeded by a long period of silence. The Germans, shot at point-blank range, lay dead on the floor. Sprawled diagonally across the bed, Morvan also lay motionless. Cousin sat in a similar state of complete immobility; he was waiting for his paralysis to lessen.

This process began with the release of his mental faculties, which gradually recovered their power. Soon afterward he became conscious of reality and was once again capable of rational thought. He realized then that the situation he had done his utmost to avoid was now even more dreadful than when he was still in the hands of the enemy.

Nothing held him back. He merely had to open the door and he would be free. Free? Free to go back among friends, to answer all their questions and tell them the whole story? It was at this precise point that something was set in motion in his mind and he understood for the first time the imperious commands of that sovereign power which, mindful of his interests, was now calling upon him to take action. At the same time he felt that the chains that had seemed to bind him tightly were loosening.

The voice commanded that he should first get out of his handcuffs. He applied himself to this task without hurrying, with the cool deliberation inspired by his urge to obey. It was not very difficult; in a short time he succeeded in setting himself free, without ceasing to watch Morvan out of the corner of his eye, without making a sound that might have alerted him. At that moment he was imbued with the resolution and calm courage of the hero who inhabited his dreams, and he rejoiced at the thought.

Morvan opened his eyes and saw that Cousin was free. He seemed to divine his intention and reached down for the submachine gun, which had fallen by the side of his bed. Cousin forestalled him. Nothing hindered the play of his muscles any longer, and his instinct of self-preservation was matched on the physical plane by perfect coordination. He leaped forward and snatched up the weapon just as Morvan was about to lay hands on it. He counted this success as his first victory.

But the elimination of a troublesome witness was not the essential part of his act. The mind makes many other demands! It demands belief in its own virtue. His own mind now demanded that Morvan be the traitor and he, Cousin, a judge created by a divine Providence. It was no effort for him to perform this sublime intellectual feat. He even raised himself to such heights of credulity that he felt the need to express himself out loud, to shout so as to convince Morvan even more of his utter ignominy.

"Swine! Traitor! Think of your comrades who are even now paying for your foul crime with their own precious blood!"

He raged at Morvan for the best part of a minute, in the grip of a fury it was only natural for the hero of his dreams to feel in these circumstances. He spat in his face and clouted him over the head before emptying the rest of the magazine into his breast.

The sound of his words had intensified his righteous indignation. At the thought of those dead comrades, sacrificed through cowardice, his anger knew no bounds. And such was the miracle of his imagination that when he found himself the sole survivor in the room, when he saw that Morvan was dead beyond all doubt and that his own voice could not be heard by any ear but his own, he still went on in the same tone.

Alone among the dead, for his ear alone, he uttered the words that put his sacred mission in its true perspective and made him appear as the glorious avenging angel:

"This is the just reward for all traitors."

32   He had recovered this same state of grace when he entered the villa at Gleicher's heels, and once again he whispered the romantic words that gave expression to his radiant metamorphosis:

"This is the just reward for all traitors."

And at that moment, just as when he had shot Morvan dead, professional artistic distortion coming to his aid, a fierce, intransigent patriotism strengthened his arm.

He knew every inch of the villa, which was constructed on the same plan as his own. The living room, which opened out onto a long corridor, was the only part of the house that Gleicher used. He slept there on a sofa, after playing his favorite records over and over again. Arvers was acquainted with his habits. In the middle of the night, he knew, he would always find Gleicher there sitting in front of a log fire, prepared to listen to the music till daybreak. He was also well aware that the German never left the house without his overcoat. He had rehearsed all the necessary gestures and now performed them with clockwork precision.

He slipped past the door of the living room and hid behind a cupboard. He had taken from his pocket the object Austin and Claire had noticed: it was the piano wire he had not been able to bring himself to use on Bergen. He wound the two ends around his wrists to get a firmer grip and tested the tension of his muscles. Gleicher was on his way back, buttoning up his coat, without having bothered to turn off the phonograph. He emerged from the room and had taken one step toward the front door when Arvers pounced on him.

Several minutes had passed since Arvers had disappeared inside, and Austin was still pondering over his strange behavior. He listened in vain: the phonograph drowned every other sound.

The music finally stopped and the house fell silent. Standing beside him, her brow wrinkled, Claire seemed to be working out a problem in her head. Suddenly she put a hand to her forehead and cried out in a tone of despair:

"The tape, the tape recording! That's what he's after; he'd do anything to get his hands on it."

Her voice rang out in the silence. Austin seized her by the arm to keep her quiet, but she shook him off and again cried out:

"He's going to destroy it. We'll be too late."

She started running toward the villa, throwing caution to the winds, and pushed open the front gate with a metallic clang that made Austin wince. He followed her, realizing there was no point in hiding since she had almost certainly revealed their presence.

He caught up with her on the doorstep. He caught up with her there because that was where she had stopped dead in her tracks, as he also did, at Arvers' sudden reappearance on the threshold. A smile of triumph hovered on his lips. Behind him they could see a lifeless body stretched out in the corridor. He pushed the door open with a sweeping, almost spectacular gesture and stood aside to let them view his handiwork.

He showed no sign of surprise; in fact, he seemed to be expecting them. He was no longer frightened of them—rather the reverse. He rejoiced in their presence here and also in his own perspicacity that had led him to foresee it. They had turned up at the very moment he had hoped—as providential witnesses to his valor.

Having derived sufficient pleasure from their bewilderment, he broke the silence in a tone of supreme detachment.

"I've liquidated him," he said.

"What!"

Austin, in turn, had been unable to suppress a cry of amazement. His nerves were strained by the long nocturnal vigil and, above all, by the ghastly sensation of being surrounded on all sides by lunatics who were trying to pass themselves off as sane.

"Gleicher—I've just liquidated him," Arvers explained calmly. "He was a traitor. I had suspected it for some time, but I only had proof of it tonight. . . . I strangled him."

He felt he was waking up to a glorious dawn after a

hideous nightmare. It cost him scarcely any effort to assume the air of negligence that fitted in with his present frame of mind.

"I strangled him with a length of piano wire. It's the surest way and the most silent."

Claire, having recovered from her surprise, pushed him aside and, stepping over the body without so much as glancing at it, rushed into the living room. She made straight for the fireplace, then stood there wringing her hands. The grate was red-hot, the logs crackling. A poker half embedded in the embers suggested that the fire had been rekindled recently. She rummaged among the glowing ashes but could find no identifiable remains. Then she suddenly noticed a flat leather cylinder case lying on the table. In a towering rage she snatched it up and hurried back to the front door. Arvers was in the process of telling Austin the whole story.

"I had my suspicions about his loyalty, but it was only tonight, when he turned up for the meeting, that I knew for sure—all he had in mind was to lead you into a trap. How do I know? I overheard a conversation between him and his assistant."

He was making up the story as he went along, like an expert novelist who, on taking up his pen, has not yet worked out his plot in detail but whose inspiration is directed at each fresh chapter by the general idea of his book: a beacon serving both as guide and support in his efforts to produce out of the void the necessary chain of events. He had recovered all his intellectual faculties and confidence in his own mastery.

"Yes, as you still hadn't arrived, I pretended to go upstairs and leave them together. In actual fact, I listened at the door. It was then I heard this conversation, which left me in no doubt as to their intentions. To begin with, I realized at once that Gleicher was the important figure, a senior *Abwehr* officer. . . . Otto?—a mere subordinate. They had been deliberately misleading us right from the start. I also discovered that all the information they had provided was manufactured by the *Abwehr*—a vast deception scheme, in fact."

Not knowing exactly how much his chief had found out, he took great pains not to diverge too far from the actual facts. What he said tallied so closely with what Austin had seen for himself that the latter was disconcerted and began almost to reproach himself for having thought of Arvers as a traitor.

"After that it was only too clear what Gleicher's intentions were. There was no question of establishing contact with the Allies. They were both sniggering at the thought of this trick and at our gullibility. All they were after was to get one or several members of our service into their clutches and thus deliver a fatal blow to our clandestine organization. The trap wasn't set for tonight, but for another meeting he was going to arrange later. There was already considerable danger in his meeting you and being able to identify you.

"I was appalled. It was lucky you didn't show up. I only began to breathe freely again after they left. Then I followed them in the dark. I heard the car. It was Otto, and I knew that Gleicher would be spending the night here."

Based as it was on facts that were strictly true, the story was taking shape of its own accord. Even if they had spied every gesture he had made in the course of the evening, they could not question a single point in his tale.

Austin would have given anything just then to have been able to lay bare Arvers' cranium and look into the tortuous folds of his brain; for a moment he felt that this was the only certain means of arriving at the truth when confronted with such a mind. But Austin was mistaken. If he had been in a position to carry out the operation and inspection, even then, in the innermost whorls of the gray matter, he would have found nothing but confirmation of the noble intentions that permeated the story.

The subjective slant Arvers gave to the events was at the same time so natural and so intoxicating that he began to believe in it himself. In the course of his description he produced a revised, improved version of reality, one corresponding so closely to his secret ambition that his mind was unable to question it. Molding, manipulating the raw material of the facts in such a way as to make it yield a satisfactory meaning—that was what he had done all his life. The profession in which he was a past master was now revealed in all its glorious majesty. The exultant sense of his own virtue almost brought tears of enthusiasm to his eyes as he gave the finishing touches to his personality by means of the skillful magic of words.

"He was alone, I knew. He didn't suspect a thing— he thought I had been completely taken in. I couldn't wait any longer; the opportunity was too good to miss. I came and knocked at the door and told him you had just arrived and wanted to see him. He went back to get his coat. I followed him inside and then I strangled him with this wire. He didn't utter a sound."

His voice had the very ring of truth, and the proof of what he asserted was there in the passage. Austin was under his spell; once again he began to suspect that Claire was out of her mind or had invented the whole story to bring about Arvers' downfall.

She would never be convinced of his good will, Arvers realized. But what did Claire matter, after all? He had thwarted her; her whole demeanor showed she was conscious of her defeat. There she stood in front of him, fuming with rage, to be sure, but powerless. Even though she still held in her trembling hands the case he had not had time to destroy, she knew she could not use it against him. Why, she had not even thought it worth mentioning! What was this insignificant object compared to the massive corpse stretched out at their feet?

Austin was brought back to reality by the first rays of dawn. It suddenly occurred to him that he had heavy responsibilities and that this was no time to indulge—as he had been doing for the last few minutes—in theoretical inquiries into the various symptoms of insanity. There were more urgent things to attend to than forming a diagnosis. They would have to move away from here; the area had become too dangerous. As soon as the murder of Gleicher was discovered, the *Abwehr* would institute brutal reprisals. Unable to decide which of his colleagues could be trusted, he gave his instructions to both of them, in a cold, authoritative voice.

"The first thing is to get rid of the body; that will give us a breathing space. It's too late to move it outside. Is there anywhere in the villa we could hide it?"

The cellar, which was half filled with stacked-up logs, seemed to be the most suitable place.

"You take him down there and stow him away," he told Arvers. "Claire will give you a hand. I'll go and warn her mother to dispose of all traces of you and then clear out herself. I'll also have to tip off various other people. I'll come back and get you in the car, which I've left outside the village. I think we'd better make for Paris."

Arvers made no comment; he took off his coat and set to work. He felt lighthearted, almost jubilant. Claire opened her mouth as though to protest, but Austin silenced her with a commanding gesture. She looked abashed, appeared to acquiesce, and went off to help Arvers. Austin cast a final puzzled glance in her direction, then shrugged his shoulders, left the house, and hurried off toward the village.

They worked down in the cellar for a long time, watching each other furtively but without saying a word. He dislodged the heavier logs while she helped to shift them.

"That ought to do it," he said finally. "The hole's big enough. Let's go and get the body."

She followed him up to the ground floor. Exhausted by their efforts, panting for breath, they went and sat down in the living room for a moment, keeping away from the fireplace in which embers still glowed. Outside, the sun was beginning to light up the garden.

"Come on," he said after a moment. "We haven't much time. Austin will be back soon and we have to have everything ready by then."

To his intense delight, he had once again assumed the tone of a determined leader. She stood up and they went into the corridor.

"You take the feet," he told her.

She obeyed without protest. He bent down, slipped his arms under those of the corpse, and started lifting it off the floor. His back was turned to the front door.

Claire, who had taken hold of Gleicher's legs, suddenly let them drop. He looked up in surprise. She had her eyes fixed on a point directly behind him. Her mother was standing there on the threshold. She had come in without a sound, and in her hand she held one of the big revolvers they had left with her for safe-keeping.

33　　　　　"It was when I went back to her mother's place that I began to feel slightly uneasy, sir," said Austin. "I'd already looked in there to warn her of the danger and ask her to assemble all the equipment hidden in the house so that I could take it away. She had listened to my brief account of what had happened without showing the slightest surprise and without making a single remark. I went off to make some telephone calls and collect my car. When I got back I found the house empty.

"Yet I had told her to be sure to wait for me. I went through into the back parlor. She hadn't done a thing I had asked. She must have gone out immediately after I left. It was then I felt there was something strange afoot.

"I wanted to dash back to the villa at once, but I had some trouble with the car. Those damn charcoal-gas engines . . ."

Austin was telling Dr. Fog about the end of his mission. His departure from France having been delayed because of bad weather, some time had elapsed since the events he was describing had occurred; but from the vehemence in his voice it was clear they had left a vivid impression on him and he was not likely to forget them for some time to come. Dr. Fog listened in silence. In the course of an unusually varied career he had come across any number of weird characters and strange situations. Eccentricity was his specialty, and, as he sometimes went so far as to admit, he felt a secret admiration for it. He was interested in the final episode of the Arvers affair but saw no reason for getting unduly worked up about it. His lack of emotion, which seemed almost tantamount to incomprehension, irritated Austin, whose feelings were roused all over again as he described each stage of the drama. He was stumbling over himself to evoke the atmosphere of that morning for the benefit of his chief, and from time to time digressed into trivial details that, at the time, had seemed of vital importance.

"The engine had conked out! Those damn contraptions they use in France these days, sir! And like a fool I wasted at least a quarter of an hour trying to get started again. Otherwise I might have reached there in time. It was only when I realized I could do nothing about it that I thought of setting off on foot. You understand, sir?"

"I understand," Dr. Fog replied in an encouraging tone. "So you set off on foot?"

"It wasn't very far. Twenty minutes' walk—not even that in my case, as I started to run as soon as I was outside the village. I was getting more and more apprehensive. . . . A sort of intuition, as I said, and the feeling grew stronger as I went along. It was the old woman's attitude I could not get out of my mind: that placidity of hers, that indifference, that apparent lack of all emotion . . . Yet anything to do with him must have concerned her at least as deeply as it did her daughter."

"Some people have a special gift for hiding their feelings," Dr. Fog observed sententiously. "Generally speaking, it's a sign of character."

"As soon as the villa came in sight above the trees, there was something about it that alarmed me—yes, that's the only word for it: alarmed me—something incongruous. A mere detail, insignificant in itself, but why did it have such an effect on me? I can't explain, but I was all on edge. It was the thick smoke rising from the chimney. The fire must have been rekindled, otherwise it would have gone out. There were dozens of reasons to account for this. They might have been burning some papers or other incriminating documents; and yet at the sight of it I was filled with foreboding. I had slackened my pace because I was out of breath; now I broke into a run again. What for, I wonder?"

"As you say, what for?" Dr. Fog said softly.

"I burst into the garden. The two women were there, Claire and her mother, sitting on the doorstep, their heads propped on their hands. Claire moved slightly as I approached. I was going to question her but I found I couldn't; the sight of her face chilled me to the bone. Unrecognizable, impossible to describe, sir. Never have I seen such an expression of horror engraved on a human face.

"I stopped dead in my tracks, unable to move, then took a step toward her. It was then I noticed the smell and was paralyzed all over again. I forgot to tell you that the front door and the door of the living room were both wide open. That's where the smell was coming from. There was no wind, not the slightest puff. Sir, if hell really exists, it couldn't give off a more poisonous stench than the one I smelled when I reached that house."

When he saw the girl's mother standing before him, Arvers realized his triumph was not complete and that he would have to face one last ordeal. This did not surprise him. He had *known* for a long time that he would have to contend with the old woman someday. Her appearance at the scene seemed strangely familiar to him. Her menacing attitude did not impress him in the least —this was just how he had imagined it would be.

"Put your hands behind your back," she said.

He obeyed quietly, but not because of fear. He questioned himself objectively on this score and discovered with delight that this emotion had become alien to him.

He did not move when Claire tied his wrists together. He only had to bide his time and wait for the proper moment to play his part in the scenario that the two women had evidently worked out in detail long before, in case all other means of attaining their aim should fail. They did not exchange a word, yet Claire needed no prompting. Her mother had thrown her a length of rope. She had thought of every detail, but she hadn't . . . He inwardly rejoiced at the thought that she hadn't, that she couldn't have, foreseen *everything*.

When his hands were firmly bound, the old woman at last broke the silence.

"Make him lie down on the sofa," she said to her daughter.

Arvers started to carry out this order even before Claire had time to act on it. As he approached the sofa she gave him a shove that knocked him off his feet and then began tying up his ankles, his legs, and the rest of his body. Stretched out on his back, his head resting on a cushion, he fixed his eyes on the old woman, who was now crouching by the fireplace.

"Untie one of his hands."

She directed the whole scene like an experienced producer, not forgetting the major role she had selected for herself. She was busy stoking up the fire. She piled the logs together, threw on some new ones, and fanned the embers into life. In a short while the flames began licking up the chimney. Meanwhile Claire had unbound Arvers' wrists. Then she carefully tied his left arm to the frame of the sofa, leaving the other one free.

He let her deal with him like a child, without taking his eyes off the old woman. One would have thought she was performing some household duty, but he had no illusions as to her intentions.

"Take his shoes off."

He did not even shudder. He knew the ordeal that awaited him. He had spent night after night contemplating it in his dreams, preparing for it, analyzing each of its successive stages, patiently eliminating any unforeseen aspect of it. Fortified by this extensive research, his mind had performed the miracle of transforming it into a compulsory formality and depriving it of all its horror.

The old woman gave the fire a final push; then, leaving the poker embedded in the embers, she turned and came toward him.

"Let's not waste any time," she said. "Read it to him."

Claire took a sheet of paper from her pocket and started reading. It was a lengthy document referring to the Lachaume farm affair, based on the tape recording and the scraps of conversation she had overheard. It was also a complete confession, in which Cousin acknowledged his treachery and underlined Morvan's heroic conduct.

"That's what really happened, wasn't it?" her mother asked when Claire had finished.

Then Arvers spoke for the first time since the old woman's arrival. His voice was extraordinarily calm.

"Not at all," he said. "It was Morvan, your son, who talked."

"You liar!" Claire yelled. "You filthy coward! I heard your voice, I heard you begging for mercy, I remember what you said word for word!"

His only reply was a haughty smile. She rushed toward him, spat in his face, and would have struck him, but her mother, who had retained all her self-possession, held her back.

"Let's not waste any time," she repeated. "So you refuse to sign, do you?"

"Absolutely. It was your son who talked, not I. I can't do anything about it."

"We'll soon see about that," the old woman said.

She walked over to the fireplace and withdrew the poker.

"Mother!"

"Let me alone."

In the short time the mother's back was turned, while Claire was watching her with horror, he furtively accomplished the first part of the act for which he had been preparing for months. He had been looking for a favorable opportunity ever since Claire had untied his wrists, and the uncertainty of being successful had preyed on his mind—the only chink in his armor that fear had been able to find. With his free hand he seized the little capsule of poison tucked away in a secret pocket under the lapel of his coat and slipped it into his mouth. It took him no more than a second. The success of this maneuver dispelled the last anxiety he had in this world.

34 The old woman turned around and came toward him with the poker in her hand. He kept his eyes wide open and assessed the quality of his own determination from the fact that he was able to grasp with incredible precision every detail of the instrument of torture. The tip gave off a white glow over a length of two or three inches. The rest of the shaft was various shades of red, fading lower down into a dark gray and culminating in the yellow of the brass handle, almost as luminous as the opposite end. He felt a childish pleasure in seeing it was not merely a piece of twisted iron, like the one at the Lachaume farm, but a properly finished article constructed and embellished by a fine craftsman to hold pride of place in a well-to-do home. It was almost a luxury poker, and he was deeply grateful for this, as though the choice of such an instrument was Providence's way of recognizing his personal qualities.

"Are you going to sign?"

He shook his head with an expression that looked very much like irritation. She was *boring* him with these questions. Of course he would surmount the ordeal, but for that he had to muster all his physical resources and protect himself against *distractions*. The contact of the capsule against his tongue was enough to dispel his vexation and restore the composure essential for great feats. His sense of relief expressed itself in a smile.

The smile froze on his lips, and his features became contorted. Every fiber of his body was convulsed. For a moment the pain precluded all thought. The old woman had applied the iron to his right foot. She withdrew it almost at once and with an angry gesture restrained her daughter, who had taken a step toward her with a gasp of horror, as though to stop her.

"Are you going to sign?"

Several seconds elapsed before he was able to shake his head—just long enough for his mind, which for a moment had wandered, to recover its supremacy, to demonstrate that this pain was an essential part of his apotheosis, and to desensitize his flesh with the intoxication of revenge.

He curled his tongue around the capsule. He had only to make a tiny gesture to render that revenge striking and decisive. He would do so in his own good time. He was master of the situation. He had won. He would never yield to brutality, not he—he was made of sterner stuff than that Morvan! The mother, his most redoubtable foe, was vanquished. Claire had already given up the struggle, and she held her head buried in her arms. As he gave another contemptuous smile, he felt sorry that she could not see him.

He was again taken unawares by the second application of the torture. Fortified in the course of endless sessions of theoretical training, his mind was taken off guard by the unforeseen: he had been expecting the burn on the same foot, and it was his left foot that received it. The spasm made him writhe in every muscle, in spite of his bonds. The mother left the iron on the flesh for a full second. Even before she had withdrawn it, his mind was in control again.

"You're the one who talked. Will you admit it?"

He shook his head in the same slow, disinterested manner. He was sorry now that he was unable to speak. He would have liked to hear the sound of his own voice, but he was frightened of letting the capsule slip out of his mouth.

The third stage of the treatment had the same result. The old woman muttered an oath through clenched teeth and went off to plunge the poker into the embers again. During this respite he applied himself to sharpening his mental faculties still further and gathering them together for a supreme effort of will. He had to triumph over his last enemy—Morvan. How many times had Morvan endured the torture? Six, he recalled—he had carefully counted each piercing scream.

Each piercing scream . . . The comparison that was brought to mind at this recollection was invaluable in helping him accomplish the last steps to his glorious Calvary. He didn't scream, not he!—he *calculated*. This revelation of his intellectual superiority overwhelmed him with happiness, and while the old woman, losing her self-possession, repeated the punishment over and over again, disjointed passages of literature seemed to unfurl in the mist that was beginning to form before his eyes.

No beast would have done that, he thought to himself. And, while the fog thickened, he saw the forms of beasts swarming around him—beasts without genius; beasts with uncivilized minds and no real conscience; beasts that alternately assumed the shape of an old witch with bloodshot eyes exhausting herself pointlessly in futile endeavors, of an imbecile girl hiding her head like an ostrich, incapable of enduring the consequence of her own convictions, and of a dull brute whose only reaction to pain was to scream.

He endured the torture no less than eight times. Nothing more could be added to his triumph. He was frightened he might faint if he submitted any longer to the mystic state into which he had been plunged by this overwhelming mixture of physical pain and mental exaltation. He placed the capsule between his teeth. As the mother lifted the poker yet again, her features contorted with fury, he looked her straight in the eyes, brought his jaws together, and in one gulp swallowed the liquid along with the bits of broken glass. He felt the jolt of the poison instantly and lost consciousness, regretting he was unable to prolong the enjoyment of his victory forever.

35   "I saw him on the sofa when I finally steeled myself to enter the room. But I didn't stay there long. The smell and the smoke . . . It was really hellish, sir. I couldn't even bring myself to examine him properly. A rapid glance . . . I saw he was dead, all right. I opened the window and hurried out. It was Claire who told me the story, bit by bit—not a word from the mother, of course—and even then I had to bully her before she would talk, between one fit of hysterics and the next.

"I didn't mean it, I didn't mean it," she kept saying over and over again. "It was all make-believe, Mother had promised. We were only going to frighten him. He was a coward; I was convinced the mere threat would be enough. I didn't mean it to go any further. I expected him to give in; I was sure he would sign when he saw the red-hot iron."

"Extremely sound reasoning for a young girl," Dr. Fog observed. "Only this time he did not give in."

"He did not give in, sir. And if he put up such resistance . . ."

The doctor's composure seemed to aggravate Austin's feelings.

"If he put up such resistance, that proves he didn't talk the first time. Morvan was the traitor. It was criminal of us to leave him like that at the mercy of those two raving women."

"Do you think so?" Dr. Fog remarked gently. "Incidentally, what did you do with his body?"

Austin gave a shrug. This detail seemed to be of small importance compared to the problem that was preying on his mind. He began to reply in an offhand manner, then saw in this subject a fresh opportunity to voice his indignation.

"We buried him in the forest. As you can imagine, I didn't think it was right or proper to leave the body of a patriot lying there like that or to stuff it away in the cellar, like the other one. I felt the least we owed him was a decent burial. I took the risk of moving him in broad daylight. The old woman had disappeared—I don't know what has become of her since, incidentally—but I forced Claire to help me. I kept her at it until she was ready to drop. I was prepared to beat her, torture her even, if she made any fuss; but she obeyed without any protest. We carried him as far as we could and buried him in a deep hole. I made her kneel by the side of the grave. I was a bit on edge, sir."

"I can well believe it," the doctor said sympathetically.

"In spite of all my precautions, I'm still afraid the Germans may find him."

"They haven't found him."

Austin looked up in surprise as the doctor walked across to the far end of the room.

"They haven't found him," he repeated. "If they had, they wouldn't have taken the trouble to send me this. Listen."

It was the tape recording. Austin heard Cousin's voice, at first with amazement, then with mounting excitement. When it came to an end he fell silent for a long time, dumfounded, a prey to a mixture of emotions he was unable to explain. Eventually, under the piercing gaze of Dr. Fog, he said stupidly:

"So it was true?"

The doctor nodded.

"And they sent you the tape?"

"With their compliments. Rather neat, I must say. Otto, I suppose, discovered Gleicher's body. He must have realized Arvers had led them up the garden path and made his getaway, so he hastened to put his threat into action. You may be sure there is more than one copy of this document. . . . But that isn't all, Austin. In the package, which was delivered to us by devious means, there was also a long letter giving precise details about the Lachaume farm incident. Otto reopened investigations and seems to have gone to a great deal of trouble to reach a definite verdict. A vindictive creature, I imagine, that Otto, and furious at having been duped. . . . To cut a long story short, it's now absolutely clear that

Morvan could not have been killed by the two Gestapo men. Do you realize what that implies?"

"You mean to say it was . . . ?"

"Put yourself in his place. He could not allow such a witness to live."

Austin shuddered. Dr. Fog gave a shrug.

"I'd always suspected that, anyway," he observed nonchalantly.

Austin, who was beginning to derive some consolation from the proof that Cousin was a criminal, was revolted by this admission.

"And knowing that all the time, sir, you sent him back there with Morvan's sister!"

"He was still of potential value to us," said the doctor, "but only in conjunction with the Morvan family. Events have proved I was right. Mind you, I couldn't have foreseen everything, but at least he eliminated Gleicher as a dangerous enemy—albeit a somewhat ingenuous one, like most amateurs in this business."

"So on the whole you find that your stratagems have culminated in a brilliant success!" Austin exclaimed, unable to contain himself.

"A partial success," the doctor corrected him modestly.

"A partial success?"

"Yes. I had hoped he would also wipe out Bergen for us, but he wasn't ripe for that yet."

Austin could think of nothing to say in reply and gazed at him in a sort of daze. This rational method of exploiting human passions filled Austin with indignation, yet at the same time he could not help feeling a certain admiration for the psychological approach. His curiosity got the better of him, and it was in the humble tone of a student questioning his master that he asked for further explanations.

"How could he have behaved so heroically under torture after showing such abject cowardice before?"

"I'm sure my fellow psychiatrists could give you at least a dozen reasons, all of them more or less valid. They would tell you that paranoia frequently entails such incongruities. They would quote the case of the coward who commits suicide because he is frightened of dying. The truth, Austin . . ."

Until then he had been speaking in his professional tone. His attitude now underwent a sudden change, as frequently happened. He leaned forward, his eyes shining, his face illuminated as though by some inner flame —symptoms, the young man thought, which in others might have indicated enthusiasm or violent excitement, but which in this case betrayed the solution of a difficult problem.

"The truth is that on the first occasion, you realize, it was only a question of the lives of some fifty people. Fifty human lives—that wasn't a sufficiently clear or striking symbol of duty to enable him to overcome his instincts. Whereas the second time . . ."

Austin automatically broke in.

"The second time, he himself was at stake."

"He and he alone," Dr. Fog agreed. "He, with that dream world of his—he, the ideal creature of his own imagination! He would have accepted the destruction of everyone on earth, Austin, but not of that fabulous being. For himself, for himself alone, he was capable of showing heroism."

Austin lapsed into a painful meditation, confused, constantly haunted by fleeting shadows that he felt were converging toward some mysterious point, and constantly disappointed by interferences that hindered the clear perception of this pole. After several minutes of these discouraging mental gymnastics, he felt the need to seize on some more tangible elements.

"There are certain steps to be taken, sir. Morvan must be vindicated. As for Claire, whom I've brought back to London and who is more or less under house arrest . . ."

The doctor made a listless gesture, as though to dismiss these unimportant details.

"You can set your mind at rest. Morvan will be showered with honors—the highest posthumous awards. I've already seen to that. As for him . . ."

It was now his turn to appear uncertain and distracted. After a pause he went on:

"Morvan's citations will be sufficiently glorious for the family to renounce any idea they may have of wreaking their vengeance on a ghost. As for him . . . No one knows his story in detail, apart from the two of us. Do you feel it's necessary to spread it abroad, Austin?"

Austin did not reply. With slow, deliberate gestures Dr. Fog took a pair of scissors, detached the tape, and started cutting it up into small pieces that he dropped into the metal basket in which he burned his top-secret papers. He went on speaking while he applied himself methodically to this task. Every now and then his voice acquired a curious pitch, which he seemed to regret and tried to correct immediately afterward.

"An intellectual, Austin—I summed him up correctly. Mind you, intellectuals are to be found just as frequently among stonemasons and professional soldiers as among artists and men of letters. If you look hard enough, you will even unearth one or two among members of the secret service. Don't you agree?"

Austin gave a faint smile. The doctor dropped some pieces of paper into the bucket, set fire to them, and watched with close attention as they burned.

"I think he has paid the price. When a man has paid the price he ought to be allowed to rest in peace. . . . You spoke about hell just now, Austin? As a matter of fact, I think there's quite a chance he'll rest in peace. What do you think?"

There was a suggestion of real anxiety in the question, in spite of the casual manner in which it was put. Instead of giving a direct reply, Austin described something else he had remembered.

"When I went back into the room, sir, when I forced myself to look at him closely, I was struck by the expression on his face. His body was hideously contorted, of course, and his limbs all twisted, but his features were relaxed, almost serene. It was incredible. His face bore the mark of a wonderful beatitude and an ecstatic smile still lingered on his lips."

"A reflection of his dying thoughts," said Dr. Fog. "I'm not surprised. Yet you accused me just now of mental cruelty! Believe me, I haven't failed in my duties as a doctor . . . I did much more for him than simple humanity required."

He went so far as to indulge in certain remarks that were hardly those of a man of science. He seemed willing to discuss the Arvers case forever. Austin could have sworn he was positively reluctant to dismiss it from his mind. Each word he uttered appeared to reveal a fresh horizon.

"I've found myself thinking about him quite a lot these

last few days," he said in a low voice, "even here, in this room, where he only made one brief appearance—remember?—but where the file is kept containing the essentials of his troubled spirit. His reports constitute an extraordinary body of work that can't be judged by the standards of his professional writing—a cathedral, Austin, a cathedral constructed in the baroque architectural style of his ideal, its walls permeated with anguish, its stones cemented together with the fierce exertions of his despair, its spire soaring toward some inaccessible star."

"Romanesque, sir?" said, Austin, peering at him intently.

"What an idea . . . And yet, who knows? I'd like to have your opinion about this: Do you regard an hallucination as a conclusive symptom?"

Austin could not suppress an exclamation.

"An hallucination? *You*, sir!"

"I saw it as clearly as I can see you now. I happened to be reading through his reports at the time. And is it surprising that he should be thus incarnated in these pages? I tell you, his essentials are all there. The phantom that appeared to me was infinitely more consistent than his material self.

"I'll make a clean breast of it. When it rose up before me, I was terrified for a moment. No one in this country has been fond of ghosts since Shakespeare, not even specialists in mental diseases; and I was appalled, horrified, at the thought of having to render him an account."

Austin noticed with increasing stupefaction that the doctor's voice, as he uttered these last words, betrayed something closely akin to emotion.

He held his breath, convinced that he was about to

hear some deep secrets, but Dr. Fog managed simultaneously to recover his self-possession and control over his voice.

"My fears were groundless, my anxiety childish. All the ghost said was, 'Thank you.' I don't think I've ever felt such professional satisfaction, and also such relief. . . . No, Austin, I could never have survived an error of diagnosis!"